THE WI

A Prospect Springs Thriller

By **Novak Sheriff**

COPYRIGHT

The Widow's Secret
Copyright © 2025 by Novak Sheriff
All rights reserved.

Contents

CHAPTER 1
The Return

Chapter 1
The Return

By the time Clara reached the turnoff for Prospect Springs, the afternoon light had gone flat and hard, the way it gets in the high desert when the sun starts to think about dropping. The air smelled like dust and dry sage, and the wind carried grit that ticked against the windshield. On the road that skirted the Silver Crown Reservoir, whitecaps chopped under a steady push from the west. Water held the town together and kept it on edge, both at once.

Welcome banners hung from the lampposts as she rolled down Main: **SILVER CROWN PROMENADE — THE FUTURE WE DESERVE.** The font was all optimism. A smiling family stared out from one sign, the reservoir shining behind them like a lake from a brochure. Below the slogans ran tiny lines of sponsor names. **VOSS DEVELOPMENT** appeared so often it read like a watermark.

Clara slowed for a crosswalk and saw her reflection ghost the storefront glass. Tired face, dark hair pulled back, eyes that had not slept enough since the phone call in spring. People still nodded at her in that small-town way—curious, careful, kind, and a little too aware of what had happened. An accident, they said. A curve near Sage Creek, loose gravel, bad luck. It had been written up neat, filed, and done.

She parked in front of the house she and Andrew had bought after the wedding, a one-story stucco with a pale, sunburned yard and two scrub oaks that refused to die. The key stuck in the lock. The door gave with a sigh.

Inside, the air held a closed-up smell—old paper, coffee gone stale, a trace of Andrew's soap that hadn't faded yet. She stood in the narrow entry and let her eyes adjust. The living room sat as they had left it in April: the couch facing the brick hearth, the low table with a water ring she had meant to sand out, a shelf of paperbacks. A thin drift of dust lay on the mantel the way snow lies when a storm can't make up its mind.

She set her bag down, then walked through the kitchen to the back window. The reservoir lay low and glassy beyond the ridge, a strip of steel under the sky. In the sink was a mug she did not remember, rim stained, spoon inside. The smallest things pressed hardest.

A knock came from the open front door. Clara turned. A man filled the doorway, hat in hand, uniform pressed, badge bright.

"Mrs. Hart," he said.

"Clara is fine," she said.

Sheriff Conrad Hale had the kind of face that seemed built to reassure, wide at the cheekbones, steady at the eyes. He stepped in, kept his boots on the mat, and nodded toward the rooms like he knew each one.

"Welcome back. I wanted to stop by, see if you needed anything. We still have property in evidence—the wallet, watch, a few items from the vehicle. We can release them whenever you're ready."

"Thank you." Her voice sounded even, and she was glad of

that.

He shifted his hat to his other hand. "If there's paperwork you'd like help with, my office can make it easier. I know how these things can pile up."

Clara almost said she would handle it, then stopped. "I'll let you know."

"Of course." Hale gave a small, practiced smile. "And if the house doesn't feel safe, we can swing a cruiser by at night for a week or two."

"I'll be okay," she said. It came out fast.

Hale didn't take offense. "Still. You have my card." He set it on the table, square with the edge, then looked past her at the kitchen window, the small view of water. "Folks out there miss Andrew," he said. "He did good work for the community."

He let the words hang, nodded once more, and left as quietly as he had come.

Clara waited until the cruiser eased away, then exhaled, surprised at how much air her body had been holding. She gathered the card, turned it over, and put it in a drawer she did not plan to use.

The day had thinned. She started the water, set a kettle on the stove, and walked down the short hall to the study. Andrew had always called it that, though it was a small room with a desk and two bookcases and a window that looked toward the ridge. The blinds were half-tilted; stripes of pale light lay across the desk like bars.

She ran a hand over the chair back, then sat. The desk was clean in Andrew's way—no piles, each tool in its place, a worn leather blotter, pens lined up in a tray, a square of sanded wood he used as a coaster. On the left, a little drawer stuck when she tried it. She jiggled it, pulled, and it came free with a soft bump. Inside lay a few envelopes, a roll of stamps, an old statewide map with the corners broken white, and a key on a fob from a highway lodge halfway to the county line—**SAGE CREST LODGE**, Room **12** stamped into the metal tag.

Clara held the key and felt the cool weight of it. She turned the tag over and stared at the numbers. Room 12.

A hundred pictures tried to build themselves at once. She set the key down, steady.

Below the envelopes sat a narrow index card with a line in Andrew's block letters, the kind of note he made when he didn't want to forget something. **Thursday — blue door.**

Her mouth went dry. The kettle in the kitchen clicked once as the first bubbles woke.

She told herself to catalog, not guess. She stacked the envelopes, pulled the map, slid the drawer shut. Then she opened the larger center drawer. Stationery, paper clips, a rubber band ball that had stopped growing years ago, a small digital recorder she didn't remember, the old house phone bill. The bill's top corner showed a list of messages still stored on the landline voicemail—eight, nine, ten, a block of them with dates in 2010 and 2011.

She stood and went to the hall where the base unit sat, half hidden under a junk-mail catalog. She punched **PLAY**.

The machine clicked, then a woman's voice filled the hall, rough with panic and breath. "Andrew, I'm late. I'm sorry. I can't do this alone. Please call me. Please." The time stamp read **September 2010**.

Clara's hand found the wall. Another message rolled in, the same voice on a later date, steadier but thin. "It's me. I told him no. I'm keeping it. I just—can you meet? Thursday? The place with the blue door."

She hit **STOP**. The hall went dead quiet. Even the kettle seemed to hold its breath across the house.

It could be anything, she told herself. It could be someone from the office, a friend of a friend who had the wrong number, a wronged stranger. It could be nothing to do with him. But the note in his drawer said **Thursday — blue door**, and the key from a place out on the highway had **12** pressed in its face, and now her own heartbeat sounded like a knock on a door she did not want to open.

Footsteps sounded on the porch, quick and light. She drew in a breath and glanced at the front door. The man who stepped in wore plain clothes, a clipped badge on his belt, and the easy tired look of someone who had talked to too many people this week.

"Clara?" he said. "Sam Reyes. County investigations. We spoke by phone in April—about the crash report, and your request for copies."

She nodded, grateful for the anchor of his name. "Right. Come in."

He stayed near the doorway, as if he did not want to put a mark on the floor. "I was in Prospect for a meeting, thought I'd see if the report raised questions. Sometimes it does, after a little time."

"Sometimes?" she said.

Sam gave a half smile. "Most of the time." He studied her face, then looked past her at the hall, the small, neat rooms. "How are you doing with all this?"

Clara almost said fine, then didn't. "I'm here," she said. "I don't know if that counts."

"It counts," he said. "If you want, I can walk you through the file again. No pressure."

She hesitated. The drawer in the study felt like a live thing behind her, the key and the card and the messages lined up like points on a map. She didn't want anyone to see them yet, not even the honest face at her door.

"Maybe next week," she said. "I've only just walked in."

"Got it." He set a slim folder on the entry table. "I brought copies of the photos, the statements, the reconstruction. If you decide to look tonight, don't do it alone."

She heard the care in his voice and saw that it wasn't just for her. He had the look of someone who had learned the hard way that paper can hit like a truck.

Sam tipped his chin toward the street. "You'll see a lot of **Voss Development** around town. He pushed for safer shoulders after the spring storms. We're all for it." His mouth tightened a little, a flash of dry humor. "After the vote, money pours through, and the pouring makes the roads better, I guess."

"You guess," she said.

He shrugged. "I'm not a road guy. I count what happens after." He straightened. "If you need anything, call my cell. It's on the card in the file."

"Thank you," she said.

When he left, the house settled again, the kettle began to sing, and Clara realized she had been standing in the same square of floor for a long time.

She made tea she did not want and carried it to the study. On the desk she laid the key, the index card, the phone bill with the old message count circled in red, the map. She drew a small notebook from her bag and wrote two columns: **What I Know**, **What I Think**.

Under **What I Know** she wrote:

- Key: **Sage Crest Lodge**, Room **12**.

- Note: **Thursday — blue door**.

- Voicemails: **Sept–Oct 2010**, same female voice, sounds scared. "I'm late," "I'm keeping it," "Please meet, Thursday, blue door."

- Andrew's calendar—check for Thursdays.

Under **What I Think** she wrote, and then stopped, because the first line would cut. She kept the pen down, stared at the blank space, then wrote it anyway.

· He was seeing someone.

She sat there with the line, small and black and unforgiving on the page. The room hummed with the tiny sounds a house makes when no one is talking—the fridge cycling, the tick of heat in the wall, the faint rasp of wind at the eaves.

She pulled the map open and smoothed it flat. The highway ran south toward the county line, then east toward a cluster of small towns. She found the exit where the lodge would be; she had passed it a hundred times and never looked twice. Sage Crest. She traced the route with a fingertip, the way she had traced patterns on her leg as a child when she had to sit still in church.

The desk held one more place to look. Andrew kept a wall calendar as well as the one on his phone, the paper kind with pencil lines where he liked them. She slid open the drawer that held it and lifted the book onto the blotter. The months lay thin and square, edges nicked from use.

She flipped to spring of this year, the weeks before he died. Work meetings, short notes, a council session, dinner with friends, nothing odd. Then she went back, month by month, into the winter, then fall, then summer. In each, one Thursday had a small block letter beside it: **SC**. Sometimes he wrote it at the top of the day, sometimes in the right margin, but it was there most months, steady as a heartbeat.

She turned farther back, into 2015, and found the same thing. **SC**. She checked 2014, 2013. The marks thinned in the older pages, but enough remained to make a pattern. One Thursday, most months. **SC**.

She stared at the letters until the two characters blurred. **SC** could be anything. **Silver Crown**, which made no sense, because you didn't need to mark a lake you could see from your house. **Supply run**, which sounded like a joke. **Sage Crest**, which landed clean and hard in her chest when she let it.

Her throat tightened. She reached for the tea and found it cold.

On the shelf above the desk sat a cigar box that held, by habit, spare change and parking receipts. She took it down and shook it, listening for the sound of more keys, a folded paper, anything that would explain what he had done without cutting her open. Coins hit wood, and nothing else.

Clara set the box back and sat very still. She let the anger come because trying to stop it made it worse. Anger was easier than grief. It had edges. She could hold it.

She pictured Andrew's hands on the wheel on those Thursdays, the way he tapped his thumb against the seam when he was thinking, the way he sang under his breath when he didn't know he was doing it. She pictured a door painted blue, metal numbers screwed crooked into the frame, and a woman on the other side who knew his voice better than she did.

The phone on the desk buzzed—her own, not the landline. A text from an unknown number blinked on the screen. **Welcome back. If you're smart, you'll pack and go.** No name, no callback. She looked at it for a full ten seconds, then took a photo and set the phone face down.

She drew a breath so deep it almost hurt, stood, and crossed to the window. Outside, the ridge took the last light and held it like a promise she didn't trust. Across town a siren rose and fell once, far and thin.

Behind her, the calendar lay open to a month from last year. A Thursday was marked **SC** in Andrew's neat hand. The letters looked plain and harmless, but the more she stared, the more they seemed to point down the highway toward a room with a number stamped into a metal tag.

She closed the calendar, then wrote three more words under **What I Think**:

- He kept a room.

She capped the pen, lined it with the others, and stood. The house felt larger than it had when she came in, the rooms farther apart, the doors taller, the hall longer. The kettle clicked as it cooled. She turned off the light in the study and let the blinds turn the last of the day into thin bars.

In the doorway she paused and looked back at the desk—the key, the card, the map, the open folder Sam had left without meaning to open anything else. The life in the house, and the life outside of it, were not the same. One had dinner and bills and a ring left on a table. The other had a room with a number, and a door painted blue.

If there was no one else, why had he kept a room?

CHAPTER 2
Dust Prints

Chapter 2
Dust Prints

Morning came up thin and bright, the kind of light that makes the desert look scrubbed clean and a little brittle. Clara brewed coffee she could taste and stood by the sink while the kettle hissed. The house still felt like it belonged to another life, one that had stopped mid-sentence and was waiting to be finished or crossed out.

She took the mug to the study, opened the blinds, and made the desk a working surface. The key from the Sage Crest Lodge lay where she had left it. The index card with **Thursday — blue door** sat beside the map, the words as plain and stubborn as a nail.

She started with the files. Andrew labeled like a person who trusted the future to remember. **TAXES**, **INSURANCE**, **HOUSE**, **CAR**, **SAVINGS**, the neat black letters square on the tabs. In the back, a folder with no label stuck half an inch past the others. It was the kind of thing you only see when you are hunting.

Inside, she found bank slips clipped together with a small binder clip, edges rubbed soft. Most were ordinary: deposits from paychecks, checks to utilities, the drift of life. Then three slips in a row from **2011**, all cash withdrawals, each the same amount, each a Thursday. The teller had stamped them with the branch in town. On the memo line Andrew had written two initials: **MT**.

She turned one over and ran a thumb along the edge. **MT** could be anything. Meeting. Maintenance. Motel. She set the slips down, pulled a pen, and wrote **MT = ?** on a sticky note.

Below the slips was a single deposit receipt for a new account, dated **December 2010**, made out to **THE MARIGOLD TRUST**, a name neither of them had ever said out loud. The amount was not small. A box on the right showed "**Safe-Deposit — Yes**."

Clara felt the small lift a clue gives, even when it hurts. She made a fresh page in her notebook and wrote under **What I Know**:

- **Marigold Trust** opened Dec 2010.

- Cash withdrawals, Thursdays, 2011, memo **MT**.

- Safe-deposit box checked **Yes**.

Under **What I Think** she wrote:

- MT = **Marigold Trust**? Motel? Meeting?

She slid the folder back into the drawer and closed it. The house was quiet and too full of her steps. She needed air, and she needed a teller with a careful voice.

The bank on Main smelled like printer paper and lemon cleaner. A row of chairs faced the window where a poster for the **Silver Crown Foundation** showed a ribbon-cutting shot of Voss holding giant scissors. In the corner, a little fountain made a sound like light applause.

A teller with a nameplate that said **M. CARSON** looked up as Clara approached. "Good morning," she said. "What can we do for you?"

"I need to ask about a safe-deposit box," Clara said. "My husband passed in April. I'm settling accounts." She kept her voice even and her hands still.

"I'm sorry for your loss," the teller said, and meant it. "Do you have the key and your ID?"

"I have my ID. I don't have a key." True, and also not the whole story.

"Let me see what we can do." The teller took Clara's card, typed, paused, typed again. "We do show a box rental associated with an entity called **The Marigold Trust**. I'll need to bring a manager in for access questions."

A few minutes later a man in a gray tie came from an office. He had the kind of gentle face banks hire for bad days. "Ms. Hart? I'm Tom." They shook hands. "First, I'm sorry. I knew Andrew by sight. He was in here regular."

"Thank you," she said.

"We can't open a box without either a key or a court order," Tom said, careful. "If you have letters testamentary, and the trust documents list you as trustee or successor, we can set a process." He watched her, like he hoped she would have all of that in her bag.

"I don't," she said. "I didn't know about the trust."

Tom nodded, sympathy tightening his mouth. "If the trust was meant to be private, sometimes even spouses aren't on the paperwork. It happens when folks are planning for kids, or care situations." He let the sentence hang there, offering her a polite story to take home.

Clara looked past him at the poster on the window. Voss's smile was perfect, his hand on a ribbon near a child with a paper crown and a shy grin. The sponsor list ran in a block at the bottom, a little wall of names.

"I can give you our legal checklist," Tom said. "And if you find a key, bring it back. We can confirm."

She nodded. "I'll look."

Back in the car, a square of paper waited under the wiper. Someone had folded it twice to keep it small. She opened it and read, **LET THE DEAD REST.** No signature, no ink bleed, just plain block letters and a neat edge. She looked up and scanned Main Street. People moved from door-to-door, a boy on a bike shot past, a woman watered a trough of geraniums. No one watched her, at least not openly.

She set the note on the passenger seat, then slipped it into the glove box and closed it with a soft click.

At home, the study smelled like coffee and paper. Clara stood in the doorway a moment, feeling the heat of midday settle around the house. The safe-deposit detail tugged at her. If Andrew had kept a key, he would have put it where habit lived.

She checked the cigar box again, then the pen drawer, then the low drawer where the rubber band ball sat. She went to the bedroom, the nightstand, the dresser, the sock drawer, the space under the socks where people hide the small stupid things they are ashamed of—a bar receipt, a matchbook, a photo. Nothing. She crouched and checked the baseboard along the back of the closet. Dust and lint, no light.

In the garage, heat hit her throat like a dry cloth. The workbench ran along the wall: a vise, a jar full of screws, a drawer for bits. Andrew kept his tools like a list. She pulled the top drawer and saw a shallow tray with sockets and a small flashlight. Under the tray, a felt-lined space held a flat black **prepaid phone**, the kind you buy with cash when you want a number no one knows.

Her stomach went tight and then hollow. She slid the phone out with two fingers and stood with it for a beat before she could move. The battery had just enough life to blink a red dot when she pressed the side.

Clara carried it inside, found a tangle of cords in the study, tried two before one fit. The screen lit: **HELLO** in a simple font. Then a lock screen with a four-digit pad.

She looked at Andrew's desk for numbers that meant something. Their anniversary. His badge number from a youth baseball league. The house number reversed. Three tries, and the phone paused, polite but firm. She sat back. The ring in the oak table caught her eye, the one she had meant to sand. Stains tell stories. People do, too.

On the wall, the calendar hung open where she had left it. **SC** marked one Thursday most months. She tried the month and day from the first **SC** she could see in **2011**. The screen opened like a held breath let go.

A list of texts filled the window. The dates were old: **2010**, **2011**. Some entries were blank names with numbers. One thread carried a single letter as the contact name: **E**.

She tapped it. The thread was thin. **E:** *Thursday ok?* **A:** *Yes. Same place.* **E:** *Blue door.* An hour later: **E:** *Room 12.* Months later, another: **E:** *I kept it. I'm scared.* **A:** *I'm here. I'm on my way.*

Clara read the small handful of lines twice, then a third time, as if the words might shift on the third pass and form a better answer. She scrolled. A final text years later: **E:** *Thank you.* No reply from Andrew logged after that. The thread ended. The phone had no photos, no saved voices, just these leaves pressed flat between the covers.

A person could look at those lines and see a secret life. A person could look at them another way and see an an emergency, a man trying to be decent on the worst day of someone else's life. The trouble with small words is they hold both readings without breaking.

She set the phone down and breathed in for a count of four, out for a count of six, the way the therapist in the city had taught her in a quiet office with plants. Count, breathe, look at what is in front of you.

What was in front of her: a burner phone used six years ago, a trust with a flower name, a safe-deposit box, and a key to a room at a lodge off the highway.

Clara copied the **E** thread by hand into her notebook, paying attention to the dates. The early messages lined up with the calendar marks, close enough to sting. She drew lines on the page until they met. **SC** might be **Sage Crest**. It might also be something else entirely. People write initials when they don't want to write names.

She checked the call log. A few missed calls from a blocked number, all from **September 2010**. The voicemail icon showed zero, wiped.

When she looked up again, the light had shifted across the desk. A truck rattled past outside; someone's dog barked once, then forgot what for.

The prepaid phone chimed, soft and unexpected. A text bubble appeared from a blocked number: **Who are you?**

Clara stared at the screen, felt heat climb her neck, swallowed it down. She typed, **Who is this?** Her thumb hovered over **SEND**. She erased the words and set the phone on the desk like it had teeth. After a moment, another message came: **Stop using his number.**

She unplugged the cord, watched the screen go dark, and slipped the phone into a zip pocket in her bag. If someone wanted to know who had the device, she didn't need to invite them to her front door.

A low hum built in her chest, a thin wire of anger and fear. She did not like being watched. She did not like being handled. She wrote in the notebook under **What I Think**:

- Someone is still on that line.

- If this is about **Marigold Trust**, the box key matters.

She meant to sit and think, then found herself in the closet with a screwdriver, working a small piece of baseboard near the back corner. Old houses hide small things in boring places. The board shifted after two screws and a tap from the heel of her hand. Behind it, a narrow strip of drywall had been cut with care. She lifted it and saw a felt pouch taped inside with painter's tape.

Her breath caught. She peeled the tape slow, then slid the pouch out and untied the mouth. A small brass key fell into her palm, cool and bright, stamped with the bank's crest and a number.

Relief flared like a match, then went sideways into dread. A key opens something. It also invites whatever waits behind it.

She sealed the pouch, set it in a kitchen mug on the desk so she wouldn't lose it, and snapped a photo for her records. She wanted a witness who would not argue with her.

On the porch, a shadow moved past the window, then a knock sounded, quick and polite like the person on the other side had plans after this. Clara wiped her hands on her jeans and opened the door.

A woman about Clara's age stood on the step in a gray skirt and cardigan, a badge on a lanyard that read **Silver Crown Foundation**. She carried a clipboard and a canvas tote. "Ms. Hart? I'm Anna. We're doing a community survey on river safety and family services. Welcome back to Prospect Springs."

Clara blinked at the turn. "Now?"

"It'll take five minutes," Anna said. "We're collecting input before the council vote. It's helpful." Her smile looked like someone had taught it to her in a mirror.

Clara thought of the key in the mug behind her, the prepaid phone in her bag, the note under her wiper. "I'm not up for a survey today," she said. "Another time."

"Of course," Anna said, bright as a bell. "If you change your mind, the QR code's on the card." She handed over a glossy rectangle. **Voss Development** glowed at the bottom in small type. "We want to hear from everyone."

"I bet you do," Clara said.

When the woman left, Clara closed the door and slid the chain for the first time since she'd arrived. She turned the card over. On the back, in faint pencil, someone had pressed small letters hard enough to leave indents: **Don't dig.** The pencil must have been dull. It looked like the words had been pushed into the paper with a blunt nail.

She took a photo of the card back, then set it beside the bank key on the desk. If someone wanted her quiet, they were doing a messy job of it.

She called the bank and asked for Tom. "I found the key," she said when he came on. "Can I come in this afternoon?"

"Of course," he said, voice warm. "Three-thirty?"

"Three-thirty."

She looked at the clock. Two hours to get her head right and her paperwork neat. She made copies of the letters she had, filed the **Marigold Trust** slip with them, and tucked everything into a flat folder. She added a sticky note to the front: **Ask about sign-in logs.** If someone had gone into the vault with Andrew, it might be on a ledger. If someone had checked recently, it might be recent enough to matter.

On the way out to the car she checked the street, then walked around the vehicle, slow, as if it might have something to say. The tires looked fine, the gas cap sat tight, the windshield was clean except for a soft smear where the warning note had lain.

She drove the long way to Main, past the water tower and the little park where the swings squeaked. Kids ran under the cottonwoods, the leaves shining on their undersides in the wind. A town is what it looks like on a day when nothing is wrong; it is also what it does when something is.

At a red light, her phone buzzed. A new message from the unknown number: **Last warning.** Nothing else. No flourish. She saved the number to a contact named **X** and took another photo. If she had to show someone later, she wanted the dates and times.

At the bank, Tom met her at the counter and walked her to a small, bright room with a table and a chair. He checked the key, nodded, and led her into the vault. The cool air smelled like stone and metal. He set the box on the table, stood back, and said, "Take your time. I'll be right out there."

The lid slid open with a soft rasp. Inside lay a manila envelope with **MARIGOLD** written on the front in Andrew's block letters, measured and plain. A second envelope lay under it, smaller, marked **RECEIPTS**. A third was just a stiff sheet of paper clipped to a folded note.

Clara put the envelopes on the table in a row and let herself feel the moment. Then she opened the one with **RECEIPTS**.

Inside were stamped slips from the out-of-county clinic with the blue door. The patient name line had been redacted by hand with a black marker that had bled a little into the paper. Dates matched the old calendar marks. A few were clipped to gas receipts and motel folios from **Sage Crest Lodge**. **Room 12** printed again and again.

She put them back in order and opened the **MARIGOLD** envelope. A short document sat inside: trust formation paperwork, simple and clean, listing Andrew as grantor and trustee, with no beneficiary named on that page. A second page carried a line that said **Beneficiary: see Schedule A**. Schedule A was not in the envelope.

She opened the third packet. The stiff sheet was a donation receipt from the **Silver Crown Foundation** for a gift in early 2016. The note clipped to it was from Andrew in his block letters: **If something happens, this starts the fire.** Under the note ran a list of names tied to the foundation, including **Graham Voss**, three council members, a clinic board contact, and a line for **Sheriff Conrad Hale** listed as "public safety advisor."

Clara sat very still. The room hummed with the sound of air in a vent and the faint tick of the bank clock outside the vault. The receipts were the kind of thing that tell a story even if you don't want them to. The story they told was ugly or brave, and she could not decide which.

She copied dates and amounts, then put everything back exactly as she had found it. When she stepped out, Tom stood and gave her the careful smile again. "All set?"

"For now," she said. "Do you keep a log of who accesses the

boxes? Signatures, dates?"

"We do," Tom said. "We can provide copies with the proper documents." He lowered his voice. "If you're concerned about unauthorized access, we can also put a hold on the box, but we'll need a court order for anything more."

"I'm not there yet," she said. "Thank you."

Outside, the light had gone honey-colored. She crossed to the car, unlocked it, and saw by habit that someone had shifted the rearview mirror a fraction. It could have been her last time out. It could have been nerves noticing things that don't matter. She put the mirror back where it belonged and drove home by the reservoir road.

At the house, she spread the copies she had made on the desk and drew another set of columns. **What I Know** grew a new list:

- **Marigold Trust** exists; Andrew is trustee; no named beneficiary on the page present.

- Receipts from **Blue Door Clinic**, 2010–2011, redacted names.

- Motel folios, **Sage Crest Lodge**, Room **12**.

- Foundation donation list includes **Voss** and **Hale**.

- Andrew's note: **If something happens, this starts the fire.**

Under **What I Think**, she wrote:

- Fire = press? Council? DA?

- Schedule A missing on purpose.

She capped the pen. Her hand shook just enough to make the cap click wrong on the first try.

The prepaid phone chimed again. She didn't pick it up. The landline flashed a new voicemail icon, though she hadn't heard it ring. When she hit **PLAY**, a man's voice, smooth and low, came out of the little speaker. "This is **Graham Voss**," he said, as if she might not know. "I heard you're back in town, Ms. Hart. Please accept my condolences. Andrew meant a lot to Prospect Springs. If you need anything—anything at all—my office is open. We're all family here."

He ended there, letting the tone do the work. The machine clicked to silence.

Clara stood with the phone in her hand and looked at the study door. The sun had dropped behind the ridge. The house held a calm it had not earned.

She took the key from the mug and put it back in the felt pouch. She put the pouch in her bag, then carried the bag to the bedroom and slid it under the bed, far back, where she could reach it fast but no one else would think to look.

On the desk, the motel key caught the last light and held it. She touched the metal tag and felt the numbers under her thumb. **12**. The room was there whether she went or not.

A car slowed outside, then rolled on. Somewhere down the block, a dog barked and then turned the bark into a whine. The air felt charged, like the second before a storm when you don't know if it will hit your house or skip to the next street.

Clara wrote one last line under **What I Think** and circled it twice:

· If this was love, it hid like fear.

She closed the notebook, turned off the study light, and stood in the hall until her eyes adjusted. In the dark, the house felt honest. You could tell where the walls were. You could tell where the doors began.

Tomorrow, she would drive south and ask at the Sage Crest Lodge what Andrew had kept. Tonight, she would lock the doors, check the windows, and try to sleep in a bed that didn't know her anymore.

In the quiet, the prepaid phone buzzed on the desk once, then again. She left it facedown and let the messages stack up like dust on a shelf.

CHAPTER 3
The Highway Key

Clara left just after eight, before the heat pinned the day down. The sky was a hard, rinsed blue. She took the south road past the water tower and let the car settle into its hum. The motel key lay in the cup holder, metal tag bright in the light, 12 pressed into it like a word she didn't want to say out loud.

The highway slid by in long, pale lines. Mesquite and low sage watched from the shoulders. In the side mirror, a gray sedan kept its place three car lengths back for five miles, then fell away when a truck pulled in. She told herself not to build a story out of one driver with no place to be.

Signs announced **SAGE CREST LODGE — CLEAN ROOMS — WEEKLY RATES** a mile before the exit. The place sat low to the ground, a U of doors around a small lot. The paint had gone chalky, but someone had swept the walk and watered a row of planter boxes that tried, bravely, to be cheerful. The doors were blue, each with a metal number screwed into the frame.

Clara parked under the shade a lopsided cottonwood gave and sat a moment with both hands on the wheel. She could drive away. She could go home and put the key back in the drawer and pretend a drawer can hold back a tide. She took the key and stepped out.

The office smelled like coffee and cleaner. A fan turned in the corner and did more for the noise than the air. Behind the counter, a woman with short gray hair and a ballpoint pen stuck behind one ear looked up from a crossword.

"Morning," the woman said. "Welcome to Sage Crest."

"Morning," Clara said. "I'm hoping you can help me with a few questions." She set the key on the counter, tag up. "My husband passed in April. I'm sorting his papers. I found this."

The woman studied the tag, then Clara's face, then the tag again. "Room twelve," she said. "We've had a twelve since before I was born." She touched the edge of the metal. "You staying with us, Ms.—?"

"Hart."

"I'm Luanne." She slid the pen from behind her ear and clicked it once. "Well, I'm sorry for your loss. If it helps, folks leave with keys more than they return them. I'd say you'd be surprised, but you probably wouldn't."

"Did he—Andrew Hart—stay here often?" Clara asked. "I don't want to be a bother. I could pay for your time."

Luanne's eyes flicked to a small monitor on the shelf behind the counter, then back. "We don't give out guest info," she said. It was a rule said soft, the way people say rules when they need them. "But I can answer general questions, like a person."

"General is fine," Clara said. "Did you have cameras in 2010 and 2011?"

"Started late 2010," Luanne said. "After a run of petty theft. Still had to run them off a battery backup that died when the wind knocked power. We save over most days after thirty. Only time we keep prints is when the sheriff asks or insurance needs a picture." She tilted her head. "Why?"

"Trying to understand why he had this key," Clara said. "He didn't say much."

"That's most men," Luanne said. She reached under the counter and pulled out a flexible binder with **INCIDENTS** on the spine. "We keep copies of anything that ever made a file. Lemme see." She flipped pages. "Door damage, 2011. Truck mirror, 2012. Drunk couple yelling about a dog, more than once." A page made her pause. She pinched it and slid a plastic sleeve out. "Huh." She set it on the counter so Clara could see without touching. "We printed this for a deputy when he came by. Said it might help with something else he was working."

The print was a still, the kind that looks familiar because most security prints look the same. Grainy, high-angle. A strip of rooms with the doors in frame. The date in the corner showed **October 2011**. In the middle of the shot, a man stood with his shoulder half turned toward the camera. Even in a cheap print, Clara knew the set of his shoulders. Andrew held an envelope at his side. A woman in a hooded sweatshirt stood three feet away, face shadowed, chin down. Her hand reached; the tips of her fingers touched the envelope, nothing else. No arms, no bodies, no lean.

Luanne tapped the edge of the sheet. "That's our blue doors, all right," she said. "Twelve's there." She traced the sill of a door that had a metal **12** screwed crooked above the knob. "I remember this night because our ice machine died and the repair guy never came. 'Tomorrow,' he said for a week."

"Do you remember them?" Clara asked. She kept her voice steady.

"Not really, honey," Luanne said, kind and blunt together. "We had a fair bit of traffic then. Work crews. Hunters. Folks on the way to somewhere else." She glanced at Clara. "The deputy who took this said keep a copy in case. He never came back. I figured the case got solved or it didn't."

"Do you know which deputy?"

Luanne pulled a page out from the sleeve and flipped it. She had written a note in a square hand: **Deputy: B. Sutter.** "He's not around now," she said. "Moved on, I think."

Clara looked at the still again. The space between the two people was measured and deliberate. She felt it like the edge of a blade you don't see until you touch it. She could show this to ten people and five would say it looked like a payoff and five would say it looked like help. Both would be sure.

"Could I get a copy?" Clara asked.

Luanne nodded and fed the sheet into a flatbed printer. The machine took its time, then pushed a new page out facedown. "Here." She slid it across. "No charge. I'll print the note, too." She added the back page with **B. Sutter** on it. "You want the old key? It's not to a room now. We changed locks last winter."

"I have it," Clara said, and set the tag on the counter. "I found this in my husband's things."

Luanne read the number again like reading it twice could change the story behind it. "You OK to drive?" she asked,

33

not nosy, just checking on you.

"I am," Clara said. She put the copy in a folder and slipped the folder into her bag. "Thank you."

On the way out, a corkboard by the door caught her eye. Brochures fanned across it—rafting trips, a barbecue joint, a flyer for the **Reservoir Days Parade**. In the corner, a card from the **Silver Crown Foundation** asked for volunteers. A tiny sponsor line at the bottom showed **Voss Development** and **Sheriff's Office — Public Safety Advisor**. The font was small and tidy. Someone had used a level when they pinned it up.

Clara stepped into the heat. The lot gleamed where somebody had hosed it down earlier. A man leaned against the railing two doors over, phone to his ear, eyes on nothing. When she started the car, he looked up fast and then away too fast, like he had remembered to pretend not to look.

On the highway, the gray sedan from earlier slid back into the mirror as if it had been waiting on the shoulder for her to come out. Maybe it had. Maybe it hadn't. She took the long way back through low hills cut by dry gullies, drove one extra turn for no reason, and watched the sedan peel off toward a feed store. Her chest eased a notch. Fear is a poor navigator.

Back in town, she pulled into the county building where Sam said he kept his office when he had to file a thing with actual paper. The parking lot sat half full. A flag on the pole cracked in the wind.

Sam looked up from a desk when she stepped in. He had his

sleeves rolled and a tie shoved in a drawer like it had tried to strangle him. The room smelled like bad coffee and printer ink.

"You picked a good day," he said. "My computer ate a report, and I needed a reason to walk away." His eyes found her face and held there a beat. "You all right?"

"I went to Sage Crest," she said. She kept her voice even, kept her hands still on the strap of her bag. "I brought something."

He cleared a space on the desk with a sweep of one arm. "Let's see."

She set down the copy and slid it toward him. He didn't touch it right away. He leaned in and studied it the way people study paintings they want to understand. "October 2011," he said. "Room twelve." He traced a small motion in the air, two fingers coming near and not touching. "Not a hug."

"No," she said. "Not a hug." Her throat wanted to tighten. She made it wait.

"Could be money," Sam said. "Could be a note. Could be a key card. We can't read the envelope, so we don't know. But it's not a kiss." He sat back. He didn't smile. "You want me to log this into a case file?"

"What case?" she asked.

Sam let out a slow breath. "Good question." He looked at the photo again. "We called Andrew's death an accident because the scene read clean. It still does on paper. But pictures can wake a dead file. If you want me to carry that wind, I'll carry it."

"I don't know what I want yet," Clara said. "I thought I did. I don't." She tucked a strand of hair behind her ear and felt the heat there. "I want the truth. I'm not sure what you can do with that sentence."

"More than you think," he said. He picked up the copy, then put it back and slid it gently to her side. "For now, keep it. If I file it now, certain people get to read it. If you keep it, you control the path. We can always log it later."

"Certain people like who?" She knew the answer; she asked anyway to hear his voice say it.

He looked at the ceiling, then the wall, then back to her. "Like anyone who checks on anything I touch. Like anyone who thinks their name means they need to know." He smiled without humor. "This is a small county and a smaller town. The sheriff's office and the council pretend not to be in each other's pockets, and sometimes they even pull it off. Other times, someone's wallet leaves a print."

"Does your office talk to the sheriff?"

"Every day," he said. "That's the job." He rubbed his thumb against a knuckle like a man sanding a rough spot. "You found anything else?"

She told him about the bank, the box, the receipts with the blacked-out names, the donation sheet, the **public safety advisor** line. She did not say she had a list of board members with his name on it. She watched his face, and his face stayed the kind that listens first.

"You keep copies?" he asked.

"Yes."

"Good." He pulled a yellow pad and wrote **Sage Crest —
Oct 2011** and **MT / trust** and **Blue Door Clinic**. "I can ask
quiet questions. That's not the same as secret, but it's better
than loud." He tapped the still. "If I run this by someone in
my lane, it will leak sideways. Not because they're crooked.
Because they talk without knowing they're talking."

She nodded. "Then don't run it yet."

"Copy that." He slid his drawer open, pulled a card, wrote
a number on the back. "This is my cell. The other one goes
through a switchboard. If you text me from an unknown
number, put **CH** at the start so I know it's you and not a
robocall or my cousin asking to borrow a truck."

"CH," she said. "Got it."

"When you left the lodge," he said, "anyone take an
interest?"

"A gray sedan looked like it might be following me. Might
have been nothing."

"Color on the plate?"

"No," she said. "Just gray." She tried to remember the shape
of the taillights and came up with an impression and not a
fact.

"If you see it again, note the plate or the sticker in the back
window. People keep their stories on their glass." He stood.

"You want a cup of strong coffee and a walk around the building, or do you want to get home before the wind kicks up?"

"Home," she said. "I've had enough pictures for one day."

Sam walked her to the door. "If you decide you want me to open a file, text me first. If someone knocks who feels wrong, don't open. If you think you're being followed, turn into the grocery lot and call. I'll be two minutes behind you or twenty, but I'll come."

"I'm not asking you to babysit," she said.

"I know," he said. "I'm saying I won't like it if something happens and I find out you didn't call." The corner of his mouth moved. "Let a man have the illusion he's useful."

She almost smiled back. "I'll call," she said.

On the way out, she passed a bulletin board near the hall. A flyer announced **Council Session — Public Comment** with a date circled in red ink. Underneath, a typed sheet listed agenda items. **Silver Crown Promenade Infrastructure—Vote.** Someone had drawn a smiley face next to it with a blunt pen that had chewed the paper. The line under the smiley read **Future We Deserve**, the F pressed so hard it left a dent.

Outside, heat rolled up from the asphalt in slow waves. A cruiser idled two rows over with a deputy on the radio. Clara kept her eyes front and walked to her car like every person with nothing to hide and too much to think about.

At home, she set the printed still on the desk and looked at it without blinking until her eyes watered. The envelope in Andrew's hand kept refusing to say what it held. She tried to feel the weight of it in her own hand—a note, cash, a key, a folded picture—and none of the guesses settled in her palm.

The prepaid phone buzzed once, then twice. She didn't pick up. The landline clicked and a voicemail light blinked; she let it go. The house sat, quiet and thin, the afternoon light flattening everything it touched.

She wrote a line at the bottom of her notebook page under **What I Think**:

- If it was love, why not touch?

She capped the pen and set it down square with the others.

At dusk, she stepped out onto the small front stoop and let the air cool her face. Down the street, a kid dragged a stick along a fence in a bright, rough line. A pickup rolled past and the driver lifted two fingers from the wheel. Normal looks like this. Normal keeps moving even when your life has stopped.

When she went back inside, a card waited on the floor where someone had slid it under the door. No knock. No sound. She picked it up and turned it over. The front showed the reservoir at sunset. The back had three words in small, neat print: **LEAVE IT BE.**

She held the card by the edges and looked at the door. Then she put the card in a clear sleeve, dated it, and filed it behind the motel still in her folder. If someone wanted her to stop, they would have to try harder.

Before bed, she set the motel key on the nightstand, numbers up. The metal felt heavy for its size. She turned out the light and lay still. In her mind, the grainy picture kept building itself, and in the picture two people stood in a small square of night, careful not to touch.

The last thing she saw before sleep took her was the envelope halfway between them, as if it belonged to neither hand and both.

CHAPTER 4
Blue Door

Clara left before noon, the heat already rising in a wavering sheet off the blacktop. The road east climbed, bent, and unrolled again. Out here, the desert didn't hide much; you saw what was coming from a long way off, and it still had the power to land hard when it arrived.

The clinic sat in a low strip mall at the edge of a bigger town, the kind of place where payday stores and taquerias shared walls with tax offices that opened only in spring. A narrow shade awning ran along the storefronts. And there it was: a door painted a flat blue.

She parked two rows out and watched the entrance. Women went in alone or with a friend. A dad came out with a toddler on his hip and a paper bag of vitamins. A nurse stepped out to smoke, caught Clara looking, and lifted a hand like a small flag.

Inside, cool air washed over her skin. The lobby held a rack of pamphlets, two water dispensers, a crate of dog-eared paperbacks, and a counter with a glass pen cup that read **Blue Door Clinic** in white letters. The smell was a mix of sanitizer and orange hand soap.

"Hi there," the woman at the counter said. Her name tag read **Allie**. "Can I help you?"

"I hope so," Clara said. "I'm here about records." She kept her voice steady and her words plain. "My husband passed in April. I'm sorting his papers. I found receipts from here, dates from 2010 and 2011. I'm trying to understand what he was doing."

Allie's face shifted the way good receptionists' faces do—open, careful, human. "I'm sorry for your loss," she said. "I can't share patient information, even about someone who's passed. But if all you need is general information about our programs, I can help with that."

"General helps," Clara said. "There are notes about an **angel fund**. I saw the term on a receipt."

Allie nodded. "That's our donor-supported fund. It covers exams, labs, sometimes travel for folks who need it. We keep a simple ledger for the fund. Gifts in, grants out." She glanced toward a door that led to a back office. "I can't share names. But I can show how it works."

Clara followed her to a side desk by the copier. Allie pulled a slim binder and opened it to the first page, a printed summary of the fund's year-by-year totals. Donor names were grouped, large gifts at the top. **Silver Crown Foundation** took the first line more than once. Beside it, small print listed **partners**: county health, a church outreach, two businesses. A third line read **Public Safety Advisor: Sheriff Conrad Hale**.

Clara felt the small click of a puzzle piece finding a place and refused to pretend it was the last piece. "Is the foundation local?" she asked, eyes on the page.

"Prospect Springs," Allie said. "They send a lot of volunteers for drives and events. Nice folks." She said it like someone repeating the right line while still thinking about it.

"Do you have records going back to 2010?" Clara asked.

Allie flipped pages. "We do. We won a grant that year. It came with a rule that we keep clean books. We're proud of that." She let Clara look at columns without any names, just dates and amounts, in and out. The numbers weren't small. The outflow looked like it had a rhythm—two or three grants a month for a stretch, then a gap.

Clara pointed to a date in **September 2010**, then one in **October**. "These would have been payouts?"

"Probably exams and travel," Allie said. "We use a code. See the little **C-T** and **OB** marks? Clinic-Travel, Obstetrics." She stopped herself and smiled a little. "That's more detail than you asked for. Sorry."

"It helps," Clara said. She kept her tone neutral. **OB** and **C-T** could mean one thing. They could also be smoke.

From the back, a woman in scrubs stepped out with a clipboard. She was in her forties, hair pulled up, glasses sliding down her nose. She saw Clara and came over.

"I'm Tessa," she said. "I run operations. Allie said you had questions about our angel fund."

"I won't take long," Clara said.

"No rush," Tessa said. "We keep the fund honest. We like when people ask how it works." She tapped the binder. "We post the donor list every year. Folks like to see who paid for the chairs they're sitting in." Her eyes went to Clara's face and stayed there, reading the lines. "You're from Prospect Springs." Not a question.

"Yes," Clara said.

Tessa nodded like she had expected that answer. "We get a lot of people from there. It's a drive."

"Do you remember a woman who came in late 2010," Clara said, then widened the ask so it had room to be answered, "alone, scared, asking for help to keep a pregnancy? She might have been in her early twenties."

Tessa looked to the side, then back, weighing the line between rules and doing right by a person across a counter. "I remember many women like that," she said. "I don't say that to be unkind. I say it because each one mattered. We don't give names. But I can say the fund helped several people that fall. Some were alone. Some weren't."

Clara nodded. She didn't want to cry in this room, where the walls knew what tears looked like and would have to hold one more. "Thank you."

Tessa walked her back toward the lobby. On the way, a small plaque by the water cooler caught Clara's eye: **With gratitude to our 2016 partners: Silver Crown Foundation, Voss Development, Prospect Springs Sheriff's Office (Public Safety Advisor), Lakeview Rotary, St. Bridget's Outreach.** Someone had polished it until the letters gleamed.

"Can I take a picture of the plaque?" Clara asked.

"It's public," Tessa said, and smiled with half her mouth. "That's why we hang it."

Clara took the photo. In the frame, the words looked straight and harmless. She stepped outside, where the sun turned the lot into a bright pan.

At her car, she found a shadow fall across her feet. A man stood two spots over, leaning on a sedan, phone in his hand, eyes on the screen, head tilted just enough to let him see without looking. She got in, locked the doors, and drove to the far side of the lot to turn around. When she pulled onto the road, the sedan took its time, then slid into the lane two cars back.

She didn't look in the mirror more than she had to. She took the long way to the highway, then turned onto a farm road that ran parallel to it and dead-ended at a gas plant. The sedan stayed on the main route. When she came back out, it was gone.

She exhaled and found her shoulders tight with a tension that had worked into the bone. She shook it out and headed home.

The house felt different in the early evening, the light less hard, the rooms thinner and longer. Clara set the photo of the plaque beside the copy from the motel and the list from the bank. The pieces sat there like strangers at the same table. Maybe they belonged together. Maybe they were only near each other by chance.

She opened her notebook and drew the two columns. **What I Know**:

- Blue Door Clinic confirms an **angel fund** with **Silver Crown Foundation** as a major donor.

- Ledger shows payouts in **Sept–Oct 2010** marked

OB and **C-T**.

- Plaque lists **Voss Development** and **Sheriff's Office — Public Safety Advisor**.

What I Think:

- If Andrew paid into the fund, it could have been help for someone he knew.

- Or he was hiding an affair and the fund covered visits he felt bad about. Both read.

She stared at the two bullets until they stopped fighting in her head and sat side by side. Then she wrote one more line:

- Whoever warned me wants me to pick the worst reading and stop.

The prepaid phone in her bag stayed quiet. The landline didn't blink. For the first time since she'd come back, the silence felt like a held breath and not an empty room.

She made dinner she barely tasted, rinsed the plate, and put the pan to dry. Through the kitchen window, the reservoir lay flat and hard as a coin. On Main, the banners would be catching the last light and selling the future to anyone who still wanted to buy.

A knock came at the front door. Not a hard knock. Two short taps, like someone being polite on a porch where they felt at ease.

Clara checked the side window. A deputy stood on the step, uniform neat, hat in his hand. Not Hale. Younger, with a square jaw and the kind of calm that tries to read as harmless.

She opened the door to the chain. "Can I help you?"

"Evening, Ms. Hart," he said. "Deputy Nash. Sheriff's office. I'm on the **courtesy check** rotation this week." He held up a card that said exactly that. "We swing by houses when folks return after a loss. Make sure things are quiet."

"Things are quiet," she said.

"Good to hear." He smiled in a way that turned up only one side of his mouth. "You got everything you need? Any trouble with people hanging around? We've had some door-to-door folks bothering residents near dinner time."

"I'm fine," she said. "If that changes, I'll call."

"Do that," he said. He glanced past her at the room, the line of sight to the desk, the papers squared in a stack. "You doing any driving today? Roads out by Lakeview get slick in the heat."

"I was in town," she said. "Errands."

"Good way to keep busy," he said. His eyes held hers a fraction too long, like he wanted to say he knew more than he should. "If you plan to head out of county, give us a heads-up. We can swing extra passes. Folks feel better when they know someone's watching the house."

"I'll keep that in mind," she said.

Nash slid a card across the gap where the chain held the door. "My direct line," he said. "Call anytime."

She took it. The card stock was thick and clean, fresh from a box. **Deputy J. Nash**. A number. A small seal embossed in the corner.

"Have a good night," he said, and stepped back. "We're around."

She closed the door, turned the locks, and walked to the study. For a minute, she did nothing. Then she took a photo of Nash's card and added it to a folder on her phone titled **Front Porch**.

On the desk, the motel still looked up at her with its grain and angles. The plaque photo sat beside it with its neat list of names. The pages from the bank showed dates and amounts in rows that didn't care about the people who had made them necessary.

She wrote under **What I Think**:

- Nash knew more than he asked. Someone told him I drove today.

- If they're watching, they're worried about what I'll find.

She pulled the drawer that held the wall calendar and turned a page with her thumb. The **SC** marks stood there in Andrew's hand, once a month or so, steady as a tide. If those marks lined up with clinic dates and room receipts, a story grew that she hated. If they lined up with cash for a trust and help for someone Andrew knew, another story grew that hurt in a different way. Both stories cut.

She leaned back and let her head touch the chair. A moth

knocked itself against the porch light outside, a soft, dull tap every few seconds. Somewhere down the block a radio played a ballgame. Life went on, as it always does, and the sound of it didn't care what lay open on her desk.

The landline rang once and stopped. A minute later, the prepaid phone buzzed. A text from the blocked number: **You don't want this.**

Clara looked at the words until they gave up being anything but what they were. She saved the screen and closed the app. Then she took the motel key from the nightstand, set it on the desk beside the plaque photo, and lined them up edge to edge.

A town can run on donations and good press. It can also run on fear. Both are easy to disguise if you don't look too close. She had decided to look.

The blue door had opened once for someone who needed help. That much seemed true. Whether help had come from love or guilt or decency, she still didn't know. She put the pen down in its place and turned off the light.

In the dark, the house held together around her, a box of air and walls that remembered. In the morning she would sit with Sam and decide how much to show and how much to hold back. Tonight she would sleep if she could. The moth tapped the porch light one last time, then fell quiet.

On the desk, the motel key lay beside the photo of names that said **We Care**. Between them, the empty space looked like a path.

CHAPTER 5
The Wolf's Smile

Chapter 5
The Wolf's Smile

By late morning the wind had a sharp edge. Flags on Main snapped like someone was shaking them awake. Clara parked near the old depot, where Voss Development had opened a "Welcome Center" for the Silver Crown Promenade. The front windows held glossy drawings: clean walkways, lit benches, couples smiling at a blue sheet of water that never ran low.

Inside, cool air and a soft music loop. A wall of posters told the story of a town that had always wanted to be this version of itself. A receptionist in a pale blouse offered water and a smile you could hang a coat on.

"Ms. Hart?" she said. "Mr. Voss can see you."

Clara had not given her name. She didn't ask how they knew. She followed the woman past a scale model of the Promenade—a small city of white blocks—into a corner office with windows on two sides and framed photos of ribbon-cuttings on the third.

Graham Voss came around his desk with both hands out. Mid-forties, good suit, the kind of tan that says you have time to stand near water and talk about the future. His smile reached his eyes and stopped there.

"Clara," he said, and his voice landed on her first name like they had known each other longer than thirty seconds. "Thank you for coming." He took in her face the way people in his line of work learn to—reading the weather before they sell you a boat.

"I didn't say I was coming," she said.

He nodded, pleased by the pushback. "No, but you're the sort of person who doesn't like to leave a question half-answered. Andrew was the same way." He let that hang just long enough. "Please—sit."

She stayed standing until he sat first, then took the chair across from him. On his desk lay a heavy book with **SILVER CROWN FOUNDATION — ANNUAL REPORT** stamped in silver. A thin stack of thank-you notes sat to one side. On the side table, a photo showed Voss at a podium, Sheriff **Conrad Hale** at his shoulder, a banner behind them: **PUBLIC SAFETY PARTNERSHIP**.

"I was sorry to hear about your husband," Voss said. "A good man. He did a lot for this town."

Clara kept her face still. "He did his work."

"And more," Voss said. "He volunteered hours most people don't see. Not for the spotlight. Because it was right." He slid a card across the desk. "I know the paperwork after a loss is a grind. If you need help navigating—permits, insurance, the estate—my office can make calls. Doors open faster for some of us. No shame in using it."

"I'll manage," she said.

He studied her. "Of course. Still—if you need anything." He tapped the corner of the annual report. "The Foundation would like to honor Andrew at the council session next week. A small moment. It helps the town grieve together. It would mean a lot to people."

"To you," she said.

Voss smiled as if she had told a clever joke. "To everyone." He let his eyes drift to the window and back. "Grief does a number on the the brain's pattern finder. You see connections where there are none. Loose gravel becomes a plot. A calendar mark becomes a confession." He lifted his hands, palms up, harmless. "I've seen it before. I would hate to see you tangled in that."

There it was. Not a threat. A piece of advice from a kind man in a nice chair.

"What you'd hate," Clara said, "is a mess on the week of your vote."

He liked that, too. "You have a gift for the point." He stood, which meant the meeting was over. "Let us honor your husband next week. I'll ask our team to send you the wording before it goes to print."

He offered his hand. She let him hold hers for the exact amount of time that said she knew this dance and did not plan to take a class. His palm was warm, dry, practiced.

Out in the lobby, a display board listed **ANGEL FUND PARTNERS** year-by-year. **Silver Crown Foundation** topped the list. **Voss Development** sat two lines down in small caps. **Sheriff's Office — Public Safety Advisor** ran in the margin like a footer.

"Ms. Hart?" the receptionist called as Clara reached the door. "A gift for you." She handed over a white envelope embossed with a wave logo. "Mr. Voss asked we share materials with families."

Clara tucked it into her bag without looking.

On the sidewalk the wind went mean for a minute and then forgot what it was doing. She cut across to the diner for a late lunch she didn't want but knew she should eat. Inside, the air smelled like coffee and onion rings. A pair of contractors argued about a bid, low voices and words clipped to fit in small spaces.

She took a booth with a view of the Welcome Center. The gray sedan slid by, slow enough to be casual, fast enough not to be obvious. She watched it in the window's reflection and turned her plate so she could eat without turning her head.

When she was done, she paid cash and walked out like she had nowhere in particular to be. The sedan had settled a block down, nose toward the corner. She crossed behind it and kept going. A man inside the barber shop raised a hand; she raised hers back. The sedan didn't move.

Back home, she set the envelope from the Foundation on the desk beside the motel still and the clinic plaque photo. She slid a butter knife under the flap and tipped the contents out: a brochure, a letter with standard wording about community healing, and a card with draft language for the council session. **In gratitude to Andrew Hart for his commitment to safe streets and civic partnership.** Her thumb pressed the paper until the letters felt like dents.

The phone on the desk lit with a text from **Sam: How'd the Voss chat go?**

Polished, she typed. **He offered to honor Andrew at session. Also offered help with paperwork. He thinks grief makes patterns.**

He would, Sam wrote. **Also—that deputy who "courtesy checked" you last night? Nash. He's tight with Hale. Heads-up.**

Copy, she sent. **Saw gray sedan again. Might be nothing.**

Might be. A pause. **Don't drive the same loop twice.**

Clara filed the card with the other cards—**Front Porch** folder. She pulled her notebook and drew the lines she kept drawing.

What I Know

- Voss is tied to the Foundation and the angel fund.

- His office knew I was coming.

- Draft "honor" for Andrew set for council session.

- Nash is in Hale's pocket.

What I Think

- The honor is a lid.

- If they're watching, they're scared of what I could say.

She stared at the still from **Sage Crest** again. The angle flattened the people into shapes. The envelope between them looked like a tiny blank sign.

The day moved. Heat stepped back a little; shade found the sides of houses; kids on bikes drew loud lines on the street and vanished. Clara showered, changed, and stood in the bedroom with a towel around her shoulders, hair wet and cold on her neck. Andrew's shirt hung at the end of the closet. She put her hand on the cotton and left it there until her palm warmed the cloth.

The doorbell rang. Then a second ring, short and polite.

She checked the window. A man in a dark suit stood on the porch with a thin vase and a card in an envelope. His shoes were clean, his hair neat, his face smooth the way faces are when they are part of a service.

"Ms. Hart?" he said when she cracked the door to the chain. "Delivery." He held up the card. The top of the envelope read **With Condolences**.

"From who?"

He glanced at the slip. "**Graham Voss.** He asked we make sure you received it in person."

Of course he had. "Set it there," she said. "Thank you."

He put the vase on the step and slid the envelope through the gap. She locked the door again and opened the card.

We're with you. — G.V. On the inside flap, in small print: **Council Session remarks draft enclosed for your review.** She tucked the card with the rest and carried the flowers to the kitchen. They were white and perfect and smelled like nothing.

By dusk the heat had let go. She ate toast and cheese standing up, then walked the block once, slow, the way people do when they want to be seen as normal. At the corner she turned and saw, two streets over, a gray car in a driveway with its lights off. Could have been any car. Could have been the one.

Back inside, she shut the deadbolt and sat at the desk. The motel key lay where she had left it, numbers up. The phone buzzed once—a blocked number—and then again.

Unknown: You're making this harder than it needs to be.

She let the message sit five beats before she saved the screen.

Another text arrived before she could set the phone down.

Unknown: Thursday. Blue door.

Clara stared until the words blurred, then came clear again. The kettle on the stove clicked. Somewhere outside, a siren wound up and fell off. She typed **Who are you?** and erased it. She typed **What do you want?** and erased that, too. She put the phone face down and wrote three words under **What I Think**:

  . Someone wants a meeting.

The room felt smaller, the air too still. She told herself to count and breathe and look at what was in front of her: a key, a printed still, a brochure that said **We Care**, a phone that might carry a stranger's voice.

She closed the blinds and checked the back door. She put

the flowers on the porch to drink the night air and let their blank scent belong to the dark for a while. When she turned off the last lamp, the house held together the way it had since she came home: bravely, quietly, for now.

On the desk, the motel key lay beside the phone. Between them, the space felt like a decision waiting to be made.

CHAPTER 6
Sage Creek

Chapter 6
Sage Creek

By noon the wind had picked up grit and a bad mood. It pushed against the house, rattled the screen on the back door, and got into the seams. Clara stood in the kitchen and watched a dust sheet drag across the ridge. A small line of white cut the water where the wind had its way with the reservoir.

She should have rested. Instead she pulled the garage door and checked the car the way her father had taught her— lights, tires, the kind of look that listens. The right front tire looked a shade low. She pressed a thumb to the sidewall and felt more give than she liked. On the driveway, near the tire, a small dark shape caught the light. At first she thought it was a pebble. When she bent, the thing shone—a loose lug nut, clean as a coin.

Her stomach went tight, then hollow. She stood and looked up and down the street. Nothing moved but heat. A dog across the way barked once, then remembered the shade and gave up. She crouched and checked the other nuts with a finger, not turning, just feeling. They were snug. The loose one could have dropped from an old tire change. It could have been left on the driveway a long time. A mind in her state could make a story out of any bolt.

She took a photo of the nut in her palm, then set it on the workbench and topped off the tire with the small pump Andrew kept in a bin. When the gauge sat where it should, she capped the valve, washed her hands at the sink, and told herself that if someone wanted to scare her, they were wasting a good afternoon.

The road to town ran past Sage Creek, where the crash had been, where people still said accident and meant done. The cut there took a hard bend and threw loose rock on bad days. Today the wind had swept the road clean in some places, then left little drifts in the shade. She slowed early and steady, hands light on the wheel, eyes on the patch where heat shimmer made the line look like water.

Halfway through the bend, the car rocked. It was only a shift, the kind a gust can force, but it was enough to pull breath out of her. She eased through, put the wheels on the clean strip, and let the car settle. At the turnout beyond the bend she pulled over, sat with both hands on the wheel, and let her heart climb down from where it had leapt.

The phone buzzed. A new message from **Unknown: Stop.**

She stared at the three letters until they became just marks. She saved the screen, then looked in the mirror and saw her own eyes too wide for her face. She breathed in for four, out for six, then put the car in gear and rolled back onto the road.

Sam's office smelled like coffee that had lost a bet. He looked up when she stepped in. "You picked a day when the copier is judging me," he said, and tried a smile that didn't quite stick. "You okay?"

"Define okay," she said. She set the photo of the lug nut on his desk, then the **Unknown** text. "Found this by the tire. Then the bend at Sage Creek felt wrong. Could be nerves. Could be nothing."

Sam didn't touch the photo right away. He leaned in, looked, leaned back. "Where on the drive?"

"By the right front."

"Could be from an old rotation," he said, voice even. "Could be someone thought it would send a message." He looked at her face. "You feel vibration? Pull?"

"Just a rock of wind," she said. "Enough to make me think about the word accident."

He rubbed a thumb along a knuckle. "I don't want you driving that car until a shop checks it. I'll have a tow swing by. We'll call it a neighbor favor."

"I can't put you in this," she said.

"You already did," he said, not unkind. "When you handed me a picture that smells wrong." He pointed to a chair. "Sit. Drink something. Breathe. I'll make calls."

He stepped into the hall with his phone. Through the glass she watched him talk with a hand over the mouthpiece. The lines at his eyes went tight. He came back and set a water bottle by her hand.

"Tow in twenty," he said. "Shop I trust will check everything without adding drama. I'll drive you home."

"You have work," she said.

"You are work," he said. "Don't make that face. You want me to sit on my hands while Hale's people cruise by your porch?"

"They did," she said. "Deputy Nash came last night. Courtesy check."

Sam's mouth did a thin thing. "Nash plays both ends. He'll tell you the weather and then sell umbrellas on Main. He's not the worst we've got, but he enjoys being in rooms where deals get made."

"Good to know," she said.

He waited until the tow took the car from her driveway, then drove her home in a county sedan that smelled like sun and old paper. On the way, he didn't fill the ride with talk. He pointed with his chin at the water when it caught light and said, "Good day for boats if you like whitecaps," and left it there.

At the house he walked the perimeter like a farmer checking fence. "Call me if you see that sedan again. Better yet, take a photo and the plate if you can get it without being dumb about it. If anyone knocks and your neck says no, don't open."

"My neck is chatty," she said. "It says a lot of no."

"Listen to it," he said. He looked like he wanted to put a hand on her shoulder and decided not to. "I'll swing by later."

He left, and the house filled back in around her. Afternoon leaned into late, the wind eased, and light found the places it liked in the rooms—the nick in the table, the clean square where a lamp had once sat.

She carried a trash bag to the study and started making

piles. There is power in putting paper where it belongs. Warranties here, taxes there, a stack to shred, a stack to scan. In the back of the lowest drawer she found an envelope addressed in Andrew's block letters: **Clara**.

Her hands went light. She set the envelope on the blotter and looked at it until she was sure it was not something else. A stamp sat in the corner, not canceled. The flap had been tucked, not sealed. In the lower left, the date: **April 12**.

Her thumb slid under the flap. Inside lay a single page, folded once. She opened it flat and read.

Clara,

I should have told you sooner. I thought I could fix it before it touched you. I handled it wrong. I met someone in trouble and I made a choice I can't explain without hurting you. I don't know the right order for these sentences. I'm sorry for the days I was gone and didn't say why. I thought giving a simple answer would be worse than giving none, but that sounds like a lie even to me.

By the time you read this, I hope I will have found a clean way out. If I haven't, then I failed at that, too. I don't want you to carry the weight I picked up. You didn't ask for it.

A.

She read it twice, then a third time, and each time the lines shifted a little, the way words do when they are true to more than one thing. He met someone. He made a choice. He handled it wrong. He didn't want to hurt her. A person could hold that page up and see a confession. A person could hold it at another angle and see a good man in over his head.

She put the letter back in the envelope and laid it on the blotter like it might bruise. She opened her notebook and wrote under **What I Know**:

- Unsent letter, dated April 12.

- He met "someone in trouble."

- He kept days from me.

Under **What I Think**:

- "Someone" = **E**?

- He thought silence was a kind of help.

The house phone rang. She let it go to the machine and listened from the hall. "Ms. Hart," a smooth voice said. **Graham Voss**. "Following up on the council remarks. I'd like your blessing on the draft. It would mean a lot to folks who cared about Andrew. We can add a line about his work with the Foundation." The voice warmed. "I'll have my assistant drop a revised card by. No need to call back." The line clicked off.

She stood with her hand on the wall. She had the sudden, sharp wish to throw every card and brochure in the trash and then light the bin. Instead she picked up the phone and called Sam.

"I found a letter," she said when he answered. She read it to him, steady, even when the lines wanted to catch.

He listened without interrupting. "That's either the most

careful way to say 'I messed up,' or the most careful way to say 'I took care of somebody and kept it from you,'" he said when she finished. "Both are true to different men."

"He was one man," she said.

"I know," Sam said. "That's the trouble with doubt. It cuts the one person into two and shows you both." He cleared his throat. "Keep the letter in the safe spot. Don't wave it at anyone. Not Hale, not Voss. If they ask about new papers, say no."

"Voss is sending another card," she said.

"Let him," Sam said. "We'll build a gallery." He paused. "Tow shop says all four wheels were tight. They found tool marks near one, but no fresh damage. Make of that what you will. I call that a message and not a method."

"Good," she said, and meant it in a tired way.

"Bad news part two," Sam added. "Nash ran your plate this morning right after you left the house. Most folks don't know we can see who queries what. I keep friends who tell me when my friends are being looked at. You're on his screen."

"Great," she said.

"Lock up," he said. "I'll cruise by after dark."

When she hung up, the house held a different kind of quiet. She put the unsent letter in a plastic sleeve, then into the folder she used for things that made her chest feel tight. She added a sticky note: **Not for anyone**.

On the porch, the light went gold and then thin. A car rolled by, not the gray sedan, just a family with a dog and a kid with his feet on the seat. Clara sat on the top step with a glass of water and looked at the strip of sky between roofs. She could hear the ballgame down the block and the low rush of wind in the cottonwoods by the water.

Back inside, she checked the locks without making a sound. She took the prepaid phone from the drawer and set it on the desk, face down. She lined up the motel key, the bank list, the clinic photo, the new letter, and the foundation card that said **We're with you** in a font that wanted you not to think about who "we" was.

The phone buzzed. **Unknown: Thursday. Same place.**

She wrote under **What I Think**:

- They want me at the Blue Door. Why? To scare me? To test me? To see if I bring someone?

The house lights went out as the grid hiccupped and came back. The clock on the stove blinked **12:00** and waited for someone to make it right. Outside, a cruiser slid by slow. It didn't stop. It didn't need to. People can say a lot with a car moving at the right speed.

She carried the unsent letter to the bedroom and slid it into the bottom of the sock drawer. Not clever. Just close. She would move it later, when she had a better idea.

On the way back down the hall, she felt the floorboard that always complained and stepped over it. Small, quiet choices add up. They don't win the day, but they keep you standing.

At the study door she stopped. The motel key lay in its place. The phone sat dark. The envelope from the Foundation glowed white in the last of the light.

Clara turned off the lamp and let the room go soft. In the dark she could hear the moth at the porch light again, tapping like a soft clock. She closed her eyes and saw the bend at Sage Creek, the clean strip of road, the place where gravel waited in the shade. She saw two letters on a calendar page and a door painted blue.

When she opened her eyes, the phone faced up. A new message had arrived while she stood there.

Unknown: Come alone.

She picked up the phone, took a photo of the screen, and set it back down without answering. Then she wrote one last line in her notebook and circled it twice:

· **If I go, make sure someone knows where I am.**

She slid the notebook under the blotter, locked the front door, and went to stand by the kitchen window. The reservoir lay black under the sky, and the wind had dropped, and the town looked, for a moment, like a place where nothing bad would dare to happen.

CHAPTER 7
Break-In

Chapter 7
Break-In

Wind ran the alleys like a bored kid, rattling lids and tossing grit against windows. Clara stood in the hall and checked the locks one more time. The house gave back the same answer it always did: not much, but enough.

She set the folder on the study desk and took stock: the motel still, the clinic plaque photo, copies from the bank, the Foundation "honor" card, Andrew's unsent letter in a sleeve. The prepaid phone lay face down. The motel key sat on the blotter with the numbers up.

Her regular phone buzzed. **Sam:** *Grid's jumpy tonight. Text if anything feels off.*

Copy, she wrote. *Staying in.*

She made tea she didn't want and drank half of it anyway. The wind eased to a low drag along the eaves. From the porch came the soft tick of the moth doing its slow work against the light.

Near ten, the house settled. Clara showered fast, threw on a T-shirt and jeans, and braided her hair to keep it out of her way. In the mirror over the dresser, her face looked like someone who had learned to count to six to put the world back where it belonged.

When she came back to the study, the air felt wrong. Not colder, not warmer—shifted. The blinds were open by one slat more than she had left them. The pen tray sat just a finger-width off square.

She stopped in the doorway and let her eyes sort the room. The desk drawers were shut, but too neat—flush, no gaps, like someone had pushed them in to be sure. On the rug, a sliver of glass caught the lamplight.

She turned and looked down the hall. In the kitchen, the back door's latch sat down when it should have been up. The metal showed a fresh, thin scratch.

Her hands went cold and steady. She backed into the study, picked up her phone, and texted Sam: *In house. Back door popped. Not calling 911 yet.*

The reply came fast. *Step outside. Lights on. Wait on the porch. I'm two minutes.*

She did what he said. She kept the phone in her hand, hit the front lights, opened the door, and stood where anyone driving by could see the shape of a person who didn't want to be a story.

A county sedan slid to the curb, then another car behind it. Sam got out of the first, jacket off, badge on his belt but not shining it around. From the second car, a deputy she didn't know stepped out, slow and careful.

"Back door?" Sam asked, already moving.

"Latch," she said. "Scratch on the plate. Something's off in the study."

He nodded to the deputy. "Clear left, I'll take right." He looked at Clara. "Stand here. Don't come in until I say."

She watched the two men move through the house with

small lights and quiet steps. It took less than a minute. Sam came back to the porch, jaw set.

"Empty," he said. "They're gone. Looks like the kitchen, study, and bedroom got attention. Nothing turned over. Just hands where they shouldn't be."

She let out a breath she hadn't noticed holding. "They didn't smash anything."

"They weren't here for anger," Sam said. "They were here to shop." He stepped aside. "Come show me what doesn't look like you."

In the study, the desk had been opened and shut with care. The pen tray was canted now that she had noticed. The blotter had a scuff where a sleeve had dragged. The small cigar box sat a hair off-center.

Sam took in the room without touching. "What was out?"

"Copies from the bank, the clinic plaque photo, the motel still, the Foundation card, the unsent letter." She checked the stack with her fingertips, page by page. The motel still sat on top. The plaque photo was under it. The bank copies were there—receipts, ledger totals. She slid the stack aside to the folder marked **RECEIPTS** and froze. A small envelope that had been tucked into the back of the folder was missing.

She pictured it: thin, cream, with a clip, the words **Patient copy** stamped in purple in the corner. She had pulled it from the safe-deposit box and slipped it in among the receipts without looking inside yet. She had told herself she would open it when she felt steadier. She had not told anyone it existed.

"It's gone," she said.

"What is?" Sam asked.

"An envelope." She swallowed. "From the clinic files. I didn't open it. I don't know what was inside."

Sam's mouth flattened. "What else?"

Clara checked again. The Foundation "honor" card sat where she had left it. The motel key was in place. The prepaid phone—she flipped it—was still there, dark. She checked the bedroom. The sock drawer had been opened and pushed shut again; the stack looked a hair off. The unsent letter still sat under the socks where she had slid it. She put it back and closed the drawer.

In the kitchen, the back-door latch had a fresh scrape. The frame showed a soft dent where a tool had pushed.

Back in the study, the deputy stood by the doorway, hands folded, eyes moving without being busy. Sam kept his voice even. "No laptop taken, no TV, no jewelry that you can see?"

"Nothing," Clara said. "Just the envelope. Maybe a few papers moved."

"That's deliberate," Sam said. "They wanted one thing." He looked at the deputy. "Bag the latch, outside and in, and the glass. No dusting on paper. If they were smart, gloves. We're not going to get a show print and call it a day."

The deputy nodded and stepped out to fetch kits. Sam leaned a shoulder on the doorway and lowered his voice.

"Anyone besides me know about the bank documents?"

"The teller and the manager," she said. "And whoever watched me bring a key into a bank vault and leave with copies. The Foundation saw me at the clinic. Hale's deputy made sure I knew he saw me last night."

Sam's jaw worked. "So the world, then." He looked at the desk. "If that envelope held what I think it might, taking it does two things: scares you and keeps you from using it."

"What do you think it held?" she asked.

"Could be anything," he said. "A sonogram. A lab result. A card with a name written in a hurry. The kind of thing that makes a meeting turn into a case."

Clara nodded once. The word **sonogram** sat heavy in the room, even without the paper to carry it.

Sam took photos of the desk, the latch, the small scuff on the blotter. The deputy bagged the sliver of glass and the latch plates, careful and clean. When they were done, Sam walked the line of baseboards and looked at the window locks. "They came in the back, left the same way. Quick, quiet, practiced." He checked his watch. "How long were you in the shower?"

"Ten minutes," she said. "Maybe twelve."

"Then they knew when to knock," he said. "Or they watched the light." He looked at the blinds. "And they turned this slat because they couldn't help themselves."

The deputy cleared his throat. "You want me to write it up for Hale?"

Sam didn't look at him when he answered. "I'll take it."

"That'll step on toes," the deputy said—not picking a fight, just saying a fact out loud.

"Then toes can learn to move," Sam said. "I'm not handing this to a man whose badge keeps showing up on donor plaques." He turned to Clara. "We'll keep this tight. If Nash asks, tell him you called me because I was closer."

Clara felt a small, mean satisfaction that surprised her. "I will."

Sam walked the house again, slower. He stopped in the hall where the floorboard complained and stepped over it without looking down. "You're not sleeping here tonight," he said.

"I have locks," she said.

"You have locks someone already opened," he said. "Pack a bag. You can take my guest room, or I'll get you a room at a place I trust that doesn't put your name where anyone can read it. Your call."

She wanted to say she would stay. She wanted to say she was done being chased around her own rooms. Then she looked at the scratch on the latch and the empty space where the small envelope should have been and said, "Hotel."

"Good," Sam said. "Fifteen minutes to throw clothes in a bag. I'll stand on the porch."

She put the motel key in her pocket and her notebook in

her bag. She put the prepaid phone, the unsent letter, and the copies from the bank into a flat folder she could carry against her chest. She left the Foundation card on the desk where it could watch the room.

When she came back to the front door with the bag, the deputy was gone. Sam stood with his hands in his pockets, looking like a man trying not to look like a guard.

"Which hotel?" she asked.

"Small one by the freeway," he said. "Clean, run by a family that doesn't ask unless they have to. I'll check you in under initials."

They drove with the windows cracked to cut the smell of dust. The motel's office had a bell on the counter and a mat that asked people to wipe their feet and be kind. Sam used a card and a calm voice. The clerk slid two keys across like this sort of thing happened sometimes and the best way to help was to be normal.

In the room, Clara set her bag on the chair and stood a moment with her hand on the back of it. The AC unit hummed like a soft engine. Sam checked the lock, then set his number on a slip of paper by the phone even though it was already in her cell.

"I'll be in the lot," he said. "Not pacing. Just close."

"I'm not a witness in a safe house," she said.

"No," he said. "You're a person who had a stranger in her kitchen. It's okay to want a car you know outside your door."

She nodded. "Thank you."

Back in the motel bed, the sheet felt cool through the thin cotton of her shirt. She stared at the ceiling and tried to give each thought a chair so they would stop standing on her chest.

When the room had gone quiet enough that she could hear the faint buzz from the bulb over the sink, her phone lit with a new text from **Unknown**: *You weren't home.*

She took a photo of the screen. Then another message: *Thursday. Blue door. Come alone.*

She typed *No* and deleted it. She typed *Who are you?* and deleted that, too. Then she set the phone face down and watched the dark circle it left on the table.

A minute later, a final text: *We have what we need.*

Clara's first thought was of the small cream envelope with the purple stamp. She felt it leave the folder again, the space it made, the air it took with it. She breathed out slow and kept breathing until her hands stopped shaking.

She wrote three lines in her notebook:

- **Break-in.** Back door, latch scraped.

- **Missing:** small **Patient copy** envelope from bank folder.

- **Threat:** texts continued after I left the house.

She closed the book and set it under the motel Bible in the

drawer like some kind of treaty.

Sleep came late and messy. When it did, it brought the reservoir and the blue door and Room **12** kept refusing to tell her what had happened inside it.

At dawn, a truck rattled past on the freeway and woke her. She washed her face in cold water and looked at herself in the mirror until her eyes stopped trying to be someone else's. She packed the folder against her chest and stepped into the morning air that smelled like dust and coffee and a new start that would have to do.

On the way out, she texted Sam: *Morning. At motel. Alive.*

He answered before the phone had time to rest: *Good. We'll make a plan.*

Clara slid the motel key into her pocket. The metal felt heavy for its size. In the lot, the light had that thin, honest quality it only has before heat gets ideas. She got in the car, turned the key, and told herself that someone had taken one small thing and left her the rest: a road, a name, a door, a choice.

CHAPTER 8
Crosscurrent

Chapter 8
Crosscurrent

Morning peeled the night off in thin strips. Clara watched the freeway traffic from the motel window and let the coffee do what it could. The room smelled like cleaner and old air. She'd slept, but the sleep had edges.

Sam texted just after seven: *Lobby in ten? I'll bring you back to the house with me in tow.*

Ten, she wrote.

He was waiting by the ice machine when she came down with her bag and the flat folder hugged to her chest. His shirt sleeves were rolled, his tie in a pocket, the look of a man who knew the day would ask for the kind of patience that costs.

"How's the room?" he asked.

"Fine," she said. "It doesn't know my name."

"Good," he said, and walked her out past a man wiping down a pickup with the care of someone who liked to keep one good thing clean.

They drove the long way to the house. He parked half a block down and looked the street over with the quick scan she had begun to copy. "We'll keep it short," he said. "You grab what you need. I'll stand in your kitchen like a lamp."

Inside, the air carried the faint, unsettled note a house keeps after strangers have been. Clara set her bag on a chair and went room to room, checking the obvious places like a ritual. The unsent letter stayed where she'd left it. The desk held its breath.

On the porch, a new flyer waited under the welcome mat. She pulled it free. **Silver Crown Foundation — We're Listening** across the top, community survey QR code below. On the back, faint pencil letters, pressed hard: **Tell us if you're short on cash. We help friends.**

Sam read it and made a low sound. "They're seeding a story."

"What story?"

"That you're on the take," he said. "Or looking to be." He slid the flyer into a sleeve. "It gives them a reason if anyone hears you ask questions."

They'd barely stepped off the porch when Clara's phone rang with a local number she didn't know.

"Ms. Hart?" a woman said when she answered. "Paige from the *Prospect Springs Chronicle*. Quick question: are you seeking money from the Silver Crown Foundation in exchange for dropping certain claims about your late husband?"

Clara stopped on the walk. "No."

"Are you aware of an anonymous tip that alleges you've contacted a donor about a private arrangement?"

"No," she said. "And I won't be commenting on anonymous tips."

Paige waited a beat, listening for something that wasn't

coming. "Understood. We'll be running a short item today about community interest in the upcoming council session. If you'd like to add a quote in support of the Promenade, I'm all ears."

"I don't have a quote," Clara said.

"Okay," Paige said, bright as a bell. "Thanks for your time."

Sam had heard every word. He lifted his eyebrows. "And there's your smear in motion."

"Is this where I say I'm shocked?" Clara asked.

"This is where you keep receipts," he said. "Let me try something."

He called a number from his phone and turned a few steps away. "Rita, it's Sam. I don't need a story killed. I need to know who's planting it. The wording smells like the Foundation shop, not the paper." He listened, grunted, and ended the call. "She'll poke the edges," he said. "No promises."

Clara went back inside and gathered what mattered: the folder, the motel key, the prepaid phone, a change of clothes, a list of things that couldn't fit in a bag.

"Today," Sam said when she came out, "you don't go anywhere alone. If you have to, you text me before and after. If you see Nash, you smile like he's a neighbor with a new grill and tell him nothing."

"Copy," she said.

At a coffee shop off Main, the usual morning crowd moved like a tide—contractors in dusted boots, retirees reading the paper, a pair of teachers trading schedules. A bulletin board by the door held a fresh grid of flyers. The Foundation's survey card had the corner real estate. Someone had tucked a business card under its clip: **Voss Development — Community Liaison**.

Clara and Sam took a table in the back, away from the window. He set his cup down and kept his hands open on the table as if he wanted every choice to be easy to read.

"About Thursday," he said. "You won't be meeting anyone at a blue door alone."

"I know," she said.

"We could treat it like a meet-and-greet," he said. "Public place, eyes on, no promises. But it's their ground. I'd rather we pick ours."

"Then what?"

"Two tracks," he said. "One: you reply once, generic. *Not safe. Propose public place.* Let them show you how badly they want private. Two: I get your phone to a friend who knows how to make old devices talk. He's quiet. He's helped on work that didn't go through Hale's desk."

"You think there's more on it?" she asked, hand on the folder.

"I think people who send texts that careful don't love leaving texts," he said. "Sometimes they leave other things without meaning to."

Clara looked at the prepaid phone, the cheap case scuffed, the screen lit only when asked. "If you trust your friend, take it."

"I trust him," Sam said. "I don't trust anyone he has to report to."

He sent one text from Clara's number to **Unknown**: *Not safe. Public place only.* He set the phone back down and didn't watch it. "Now we wait. They'll hate that."

The reply arrived in less than a minute: *No crowd. Thursday night. If you want answers.* Then a second line: *You want the truth about Andrew? Come alone.*

Clara stared at the words until they stopped being bait and went back to being letters. "They know how to pick a lock," she said. "They know how to pick a sentence."

Sam slipped the prepaid into an envelope and wrote **Property — CH** across it. "I'll get this moving now." He looked like he was about to add a warning and decided against it. "I'll be back in twenty. Stay in the room. If anyone sits down uninvited, yell. People here love to help with a scene."

When he left, Clara watched the door, the glass, the gray sedan that slid by and didn't stop. On the wall, a framed photo showed a Reservoir Days parade from five years back —kids in paper crowns, a banner with the Promenade logo, Voss smiling in a sun-bleached hat. Sheriff Hale stood one step back, a hand half raised.

Her phone buzzed on the table. **Unknown** again: *We'll make* *it easy. After dark. No phones. No cop. Bring what you have.* A beat, then: *It's what he wanted.*

She typed, *He who?* Then deleted it. She typed, *Name the place,* and deleted that. She set the phone down and told herself names could wait until she had leverage.

Sam came back with a small cardboard box and a calm face. "Friend took the device," he said. "No promises, but if there's a hidden card or a deleted cache with a pulse, he'll find it."

Clara nodded. "I got another message. No phones, no cop, bring what I have."

"Of course they want you without witnesses," he said. "And of course they want you to bring the one thing you shouldn't."

She opened the folder enough to see the edges of her life. "If the stolen envelope held the patient name, we need another way to prove it without giving them a target."

"We will," Sam said. "Paper leaves trails. People leave bigger ones."

A man at the door raised his phone and took a photo of the room like he was testing the angle. Sam watched without turning his head. "We're done here," he said. "Let's get you someplace less exposed."

They stepped into the light. The gray sedan waited half a block down, engine off, a driver shaded by the visor. Sam put a hand on Clara's elbow and turned them the other way. "Walk like we're late to something boring," he said.

They cut behind the library and came out near a small park with a fountain that had never quite worked. On the far side, a bulletin board held a fresh notice: **Council Session — Public Comment — Wednesday, 7 p.m.** Someone had circled **Silver Crown Promenade** with a thick red marker that had bled through.

Sam swore under his breath. "They moved the session up a day."

"What does that do?" Clara asked.

"Keeps the timeline tight," he said. "Less time for questions, fewer surprises. If they can get the vote done, the rest looks like sour grapes."

"Then we need a surprise," she said.

"We need something that doesn't look like a stunt," he said. "Let me work."

They crossed to his car. He drove the back streets and deposited her at the motel with a two-finger salute. "Door locked, chain on. I'll swing past after dusk. If **Unknown** pings you, send me the exact words. Don't answer right away. Make them sweat."

The afternoon slid by in fits. Paige from the *Chronicle* left a second voicemail asking for "balance." The Foundation's account posted a sunny photo of volunteers loading bottled water into a pickup, **#WeBuildTogether** riding the caption. The comments were kind and sharp in equal measure.

Clara tried to read, couldn't, and cleaned the motel room

instead—stacked the magazines, folded the blanket, wiped the counter with a paper towel she didn't trust. In the drawer, the motel Bible lay beside her notebook like a joke that wouldn't land.

Near five, a knock sounded—two taps, quick and polite. Clara checked the peephole. Deputy Nash stood on the small stoop, hat in hand, face wearing the same half-smile from her porch.

She opened the door to the chain. "Deputy."

"Evening, Ms. Hart," he said. "Heard you had a tough night." He tilted his head toward the parking lot like it was the kind of place stories gather. "You doing all right?"

"I'm fine," she said.

"Glad to hear it," he said. "I'm on motel watch this week. Lot of out-of-towners with the council session up. Thought I'd say hello. If you see anyone hanging around who shouldn't be, give us a ring." He lifted a card, the same thick stock. "My direct line."

"I have it," she said.

"Good," he said. He leaned a fraction closer. "You know, there's talk about you asking folks for money. It's not my business. Just—rumors go down easier if you don't give them a spoon."

Clara let the words sit between them until they wilted. "Is that advice?"

"Friendly kind," he said. "We all want the best for Prospect."

"Me too," she said, and closed the door.

She texted Sam: *Nash at my door. Rumor drop. Same card.*

Sam: *Copy. Lock up. I'm five minutes.*

She slid the chain and sat on the edge of the bed. The phone lit again with **Unknown**: *Thursday. 9 p.m. Blue door. Come alone.*

She let the message rest, then forwarded a screenshot to Sam without a caption. Her thumb hovered over the keyboard. She typed *Name the risk,* then deleted it. She typed *Not safe,* and let it sit unsent.

A minute later, Sam knocked, gave his name, and stepped inside. "We'll answer when we're ready," he said, reading her face. "They think they own the clock. They don't."

He sat in the room's one chair, elbows on knees. He looked tired in a way he didn't let other people see. "I'm going to run upstairs," he said, meaning the county office, the state contacts, the lawyer he trusted two towns over. "Not to Hale. To people who don't owe him. I'll keep your name out of any email I can."

"Go," she said. "I'll be fine."

"You'll text me if anything twitches," he said. "I want to be the first person to annoy you."

When he left, the room settled into its hum. The AC cycled. A couple argued two doors down in the flat way couples argue when the fight is old. Clara lay back and stared at the ceiling and let the minutes pass like small boats.

Sam (brief)

The county hallway smelled like wax and history. Sam moved fast without looking like he was moving fast. In his head, he laid the pieces out: Andrew's accident that wasn't, the clinic receipts, the trust, the motel still, the stolen envelope, the texts. Hale's name on every plaque that mattered. Voss's hand on every ribbon.

He stopped at a door with no name on it and knocked twice. Lou opened it—a tech in a plaid shirt with eyes that didn't miss much. "Got your toy," Lou said. He held up the prepaid phone like a museum piece. "Hidden microSD. Locked folder. Could be junk, could be gold. Give me until morning and don't call me on my work phone."

"Do what you can," Sam said. "If it sings, I want to hear the first note."

Lou grinned. "You'll owe me a burrito."

Back in his office, Sam called a number that never made it into his report templates. "Marla," he said when the lawyer picked up. "Hypothetical. Widow is being steered into a meeting. Strong reason to think the steerers wear badges or checks with nice logos. I want cover that doesn't go through the sheriff."

"Bring me what you have," Marla said. "If I can't keep it clean, I'll tell you before we touch it."

Sam ended the call and stood by the window. Below, a cruiser rolled by at the speed of a man who wanted to be seen without stopping. He imagined Nash's grin and filed it away like a splinter he'd pull later.

He texted Clara: *Phone is in good hands. If they push again, let them. We'll set the terms.*

Clara sat up when the phone buzzed. **Unknown:** *No phones. No cop. Last chance.*

She typed, *Not safe. Public place or no deal.* Then she waited with the cursor blinking, its tiny pulse like a heartbeat. She deleted the message and sent nothing. A choice is sometimes the hole you leave where a word could be.

Down on Main, the *Chronicle*'s website posted a short "community interest" item with a photo of the council chamber. The last line read: *Sources say some residents are seeking private assurances from project partners.* The comments did the rest.

Clara closed the page and stared at the motel ceiling until the hum of the AC turned into a dull chant. She thought of Andrew writing her name on an envelope and not sealing it. She thought of a thin cream packet with a purple stamp. She thought of a door painted blue and the space between two people in a frame.

The night came on slow. Sam texted: *I'll be in the lot for a while. Don't worry about the light in my car. I read like that.*

She smiled despite herself and turned off the lamp. Shadows settled where they were told. She lay quiet and listened for the knock that didn't come.

Around ten, footsteps passed and kept moving. At eleven, a motorcycle stitched the freeway and was gone. At midnight, her phone lit with a clip from Sam: a photo of a plate number on a gray sedan. *Friend of ours,* he wrote. *Goes by three different registrations. Working on the owner.*

Clara typed, *You should sleep,* and erased it. She typed, *Thank you,* and let that one stand.

She put the phone on the table and looked at the dark circle it made. Tomorrow, Sam's friend might find something in the phone's small heart. Or he wouldn't, and they would make do with what people had left in their wake.

She wrote in her notebook by the lamp's thin light:

- **Smear begins:** reporter call; Foundation flyer with pencil note.

- **Pressure:** Nash at motel; moved council session to Wednesday.

- **Unknown texts:** Thursday, 9 p.m., Blue Door. Alone.

- **Action:** Phone to Sam's friend; we set terms; do not bring originals anywhere.

She closed the notebook and slid it back into the drawer. The room hummed, steady as a fridge, like a promise that wasn't one.

Outside, a car door shut, then opened, then shut again. Sam's light went off. The gray sedan did not pass. The motel kept its secrets.

Clara lay on her side and watched the thin line of light under the door until her eyes blurred. When she slept, the blue door waited where she had left it—in a hallway with numbers that didn't want to add up, a key with Room **12** pressed into it, a promise written in letters that could mean two different lives.

CHAPTER 9
The Ledger

Chapter 9
The Ledger

B y late morning the motel air had lost the night's cool. Clara stood by the window with a second cup of coffee and watched trucks spool onto the freeway, each with a reason to be somewhere else. Her phone buzzed.

Sam: *Lobby in five. Got movement.*

She put the folder against her chest and went down.

Sam waited by the ice machine with a paper bag and a look that said he had slept in pieces. "Two things," he said as they walked to the car. "Lou has something. And Marla drew up a preservation notice."

"What kind?"

"For the bank," he said. "Safe-deposit access logs and any camera stills from the vault lobby. We can't get copies yet, but we can make sure nothing 'expires' by accident."

They drove to the county building first. In a small room with no name on the door, Lou set a laptop on a rolling cart and clicked a file. "Hidden microSD," he said. "Folder marked **LDG**. Encryption was cheap. Timestamps say **March 2016**." He slid a small recorder across the table. "Listen."

Static, a room's air, and then a man's voice, smooth and clipped. **Voss**. Clara didn't need a name to know it.

…we can't have noise right now. Council's tight. If he's going to wander—

Another voice came in low. **Hale**. You could hear the badge even when you couldn't see it.

Conrad will handle it.

A third man cleared his throat, took a breath, and never found a word. Chairs scraped. Someone tapped a pen. The file ended on the quick scrape of a door.

Clara let out the air she'd held.

Lou leaned back. "There's more. Same day. They kept the phone near the door on a coat rack or something." He clicked the next file.

—no, he's solid. He won't talk.
He's a planner, Voss said. *Planners panic when the plan breaks. Odds are he breaks quiet.*
Odds aren't a plan, Hale said. *You said tight. I'll keep it tight.*

The second clip cut there.

Clara's pulse thumped in her throat. "How clean is this?" she asked.

"As clean as an ugly room gets," Lou said. "Same device made both files. Timestamps match the metadata. I can testify chain-of-custody from the moment it hit my hands. But before that, back this up in three places and get it off any drive Hale can touch."

"We'll route it to Marla," Sam said. "And one copy off-site."

Lou tapped the laptop. "There's also a photo dump— blurry shots of a council anteroom, a stack of folders with

Promenade stamped on the spine, a board with sticky notes. Most of it's junk. One image shows a calendar page with **Mar 3 — Civic Rm** and three sets of initials: **GV / CH / BS.**"

"**B. Sutter,**" Clara said before she could stop herself. "The deputy from the lodge note."

Lou nodded. "Could be. The image is low-res. I'll pull what I can, but don't build a mansion on a shadow."

When they stepped back into the hallway, Sam checked the corners the way he always did. "Marla's office is ten minutes," he said. "Then the bank."

Marla kept a narrow office with a clean desk and a plant that refused to die. She listened to the audio twice, still as a held breath. "You'll want an affidavit from Lou," she said at last. "And a copy under attorney custody. We'll send a letter to the *Chronicle* to put them on notice, in case they help launder a spin. No press release. We don't tip a hive with a broom."

"What about the bank log?" Clara asked.

"I've sent a preservation notice," Marla said, sliding a printed copy across. "No release without a court order. We can file for one if the bank balks. My guess? They'll cooperate once they see the names you're protecting it from." She glanced at Sam. "Don't take a victory lap yet. This is leverage, not a finish line."

Sam signed where she pointed. Clara did, too, hand steady. When they walked out, the sun hit like a hand.

Tom at the bank looked relieved to have paper to point to. "We'll lock the log and the lobby footage," he said softly. "No one touches them without counsel present. If anyone asks what you asked for, I'll say I can't discuss it." He slid a small notebook across the counter. "Meanwhile—Andrew's box sign-in sheet shows his accesses. We're allowed to confirm that to a spouse. Names of others are redacted."

The page bore date columns in neat rows. **2010–2016**, one entry most months. In **March 2016**, two entries sat a week apart. The second had a faint smudge in the signature block below Andrew's name, heavy enough to leave a gray ghost.

"What's that?" Clara asked.

"Another signer's block," Tom said. "We black out names for privacy. The pressure mark sometimes shows through." He looked up with an apologetic smile. "We use better pens now."

"Do you keep a manual log at the vault door?" Sam asked. "A clipboard, sign in time, that sort of thing?"

"We did in 2016," Tom said. "We kept it three years." He grimaced. "Which means we might not have it now. But I'll check a box in the back labeled **Old** the way only banks can label a thing."

Clara thanked him. On the way out she pulled her notebook and drew the columns she trusted.

What I Know

- Audio from March 2016: Voss and Hale; "**Conrad**

will handle it."

- Lou can testify to device and chain.

- Bank logs show Andrew visited the box twice in March 2016.

What I Think

- Second visit ties to that meeting.

- The missing **Patient copy** linked to someone they wanted gone.

She closed the notebook and slid it under the folder. The paper felt heavier than it was.

They ate late at a counter where the waitress called everyone honey. Sam kept his voice low. "Tonight's council session is moved up. I want you in the gallery, near the aisle, not the mic. Let me take the mic if we need a public note."

"What would you say?"

"That we've preserved evidence and asked for a review outside Hale's office," he said. "No names. Enough to put ice in a man's glass."

"And the **Unknown** meeting?" she asked.

"Not until we control the ground," he said. "If they want dark and alone, they can want it longer."

Clara nodded. *Control* felt like a word that had been left in the sun too long. It still mattered.

The council chamber smelled like dust and varnish. The **Promenade** banner hung along the back wall as if it had always been there. Voss stood near the dais, shoulders easy, voice low. Sheriff Hale took a place where he could see the room and be seen. Paige from the *Chronicle* leaned on the rail with a notepad and a smile that didn't need help.

Clara sat near the aisle as planned. Sam stood behind her, one row up, a steady weight at her shoulder without touching. The room filled with a mix of regulars and people who had never come to a meeting before in their lives.

The chair called the session to order. Early items slid by. When the Promenade line came up, Voss stepped to the mic with a binder that matched the banners.

"Before public comment," he said, "I'd like to honor a citizen whose work made our roads safer." He nodded toward the back. "Andrew Hart's service to this town was a model for us all."

Heads turned. Clara felt heat climb her throat. Sam leaned close enough for her to hear, not close enough for anyone to notice. "Breathe," he said.

Voss read a paragraph about community and safety and carrying light. The words were smooth. They carried no weight.

Public comment opened. A man from the chamber of commerce praised the jobs. A teacher asked about crossing guards. A woman from the Rotary read a letter. Paige's pen moved.

Sam waited until three speakers had gone. Then he walked to the mic with his badge on the belt and nothing in his hands. "Sam Reyes, county investigations," he said. "I'm here as a resident." He let the room settle. "I want the record to note that my office has received material related to a past incident near the reservoir. We've preserved it and referred parts of it to counsel outside the sheriff's chain. This has no bearing on tonight's vote," he said, and let that line sit in the air just long enough, "but it bears on how we do business."

Voss's jaw did a thing that would not show in a photo. Hale's eyes found Clara, then moved on.

Sam thanked the chair and stepped back. He didn't look at Clara on his way to the aisle. He didn't need to.

The vote got moved to the end of the agenda. The room shifted in its seat.

Clara stared at the banner and tried to make the blue on it match the door in her head. It didn't. The door in her head had metal numbers and a draft and the sound of someone breathing on the other side.

Her phone buzzed: **Unknown.** *You don't want that vote. Blue door. Tonight.*

She forwarded the screen to Sam. He didn't answer. He didn't need to.

They left before the vote and walked the long way to the car. The gray sedan idled at the far end of the block. Sam put his hand on the roof and watched the street in the window's faint mirror.

"My friend found an ID on the plate," he said. "Shell company, out-of-state mailbox. Nash has run it three times. He's pretending he isn't looking."

"What now?" Clara asked.

"We set a meeting," he said. "Our place. Our time. Our eyes." He met her look. "No blue door tonight."

"Agreed," she said, though the word felt like it pulled against a current. "What about the ledger?"

"Tom's looking for the old clipboard," Sam said. "If we get it, it might give us a timestamp we can triangulate with the audio. If we don't, we still have the bank log and the clips."

Clara slid into the seat and set the folder on her lap. On top lay Andrew's neat calendar pages, the marks that kept showing up once a month: **SC**. She traced one with a fingertip. The letters stayed stubborn.

Back at the motel, they worked across the small table. Sam copied the audio to two drives and sealed one in an envelope for Marla. He drafted a short memo to attach to the preservation letter and slid it to Clara.

If anything happens to either of us, he wrote at the bottom, **this goes wide.**

She added her initials and the date.

Her phone buzzed again. **Unknown:** *You missed your chance. Next time, no choice.*

She looked at the screen until the words turned back into shapes. "They're pushing," she said.

"Good," Sam said. "Pushing people make mistakes."

Clara pulled her notebook and drew the columns.

What I Know

- Audio: **"Conrad will handle it"**; second clip; March 2016.

- Bank: two box visits in March 2016; second entry a week later.

- Council: session moved up; Sam flagged evidence on record.

What I Think

- Meeting on March 3 ties to the second box visit.

- The missing envelope named a person; they took it to erase a line, not a name.

She closed the book and sat with her hands flat on the table until they stopped wanting to shake.

Sam looked at the clock. "I'll sit the lot again," he said. "Sleep if you can. If **Unknown** pings you, send me the words and put the phone in the drawer."

"Okay," she said.

When the door latched behind him, the room seemed to float for a second, as if someone had taken a hand away.

Clara set the motel key on the table, numbers up. The Room **12** stamp looked plain and harmless in the lamplight.

She turned out the light and lay down. The AC hummed. A car door shut and opened and shut again. Somewhere, a flag snapped once, then forgot what it was doing.

Sleep pulled at her. Behind her eyes the blue door stood where it always did, patient and sure, and a voice said from the far end of a room, in a tone that meant to end a conversation: **Conrad will handle it.**

CHAPTER 10
The River Vote

Chapter 10
The River Vote

B y late afternoon the sky had that scrubbed look the wind leaves behind. Clara sat in the passenger seat while Sam eased the sedan into a spot a block from the council building. The Promenade banners hung straight for once. People moved toward the doors in small knots—work shirts, sundresses, a few blazers—all carrying their own reasons.

Sam killed the engine and rested his hands on the wheel. "Same plan," he said. "You sit near the aisle. I stand a row up. If something turns, we step outside first and talk where the room can't overhear."

Clara nodded. She kept the flat folder under her arm like a shield. "And the blue door?"

"Tomorrow if at all," he said. "Only on our terms. If we don't like the terms, we don't go."

Inside, the room smelled like varnish and old dust. The banner for **Silver Crown Promenade** looked like it had been ironed for company. Paige from the *Chronicle* hovered by the rail with her notepad and a face that could be friendly or not; it depended on the quote. Sheriff Hale took a place along the side wall, hands folded, eyes moving without being busy. Voss worked the room in a close circle near the dais, shaking hands as if each palm held a switch he could flip.

Clara took her seat near the aisle. Sam stood behind her, one row up, his jacket off, badge on his belt but not shining it around. The gavel tapped and the chair called the session to order.

Early items moved fast. When the Promenade line came up, Voss took the mic with a binder that matched the banners. He spoke in clean sentences that didn't cost him anything —jobs, a walkable future, a place for kids to take pictures at sunset. Clara watched people in the rows nod on schedule.

Public comment opened. A retiree talked about property values. A teen asked about a skate spot. A nurse said the ER was understaffed already. The room swayed between hope and worry like a boat that hadn't decided which shore it wanted.

Paige found a moment to lean near Clara's row. "Ms. Hart," she whispered, "off the record, are you satisfied with the Foundation's plan to honor your husband?"

Clara looked at her and didn't answer. Paige's pen paused, then moved anyway.

A councilmember named Ortega asked about flood risk near the new promenade steps. Voss had an answer. He always did. Hale never spoke. He didn't have to. The lines ran through him whether his mouth was open or not.

The chair moved toward the roll call. Sam's hand touched the seat back by Clara's shoulder—not a signal, a presence. Before the roll call could begin, a woman in the third row stood and asked to be heard. She ran a small shop on Main. "I want it," she said, nodding at the banner. "But I don't want to be told later I wanted the wrong thing." She sat. The room breathed.

The chair took a beat and moved the vote to the end of the

agenda. The room changed shape in a subtle way, as if the walls had leaned in to listen.

Clara's phone buzzed in her bag. **Unknown:** *You don't want that vote. 9 p.m. Thursday. Blue door. Alone.*

She didn't look back. She slid the message to Sam without turning her head. His hand on the seat back stilled.

When public comment closed, the chair opened the floor to "brief remarks." Sam stepped to the mic with nothing in his hands. He kept his voice even. "For the record, my office has preserved material related to a past incident at the reservoir," he said. "We've referred parts of it to outside counsel. This bears on how we handle trust and process. That's all." He thanked the chair and sat.

Voss's smile held, but something behind it set. Hale's gaze drifted past Clara and away as if the wall had said her name.

They waited out three zoning amendments and a discussion about a dog park. The vote finally came back around. The chair called it. A yes. A yes. A no. A yes. A pause. A no. Three to two. Then the chair, breaking the tie the way chairs do in a town that likes order: "Yes."

Applause broke like a light rain. Some clapped because they meant it. Some because the room told them to.

Outside, the air felt thinner. Voss shook hands on the steps, the binder tucked under his arm like a flag he didn't want to wave too high. Paige angled for a quote and got one; her pen knew when to write and when to pretend it was thinking.

Hale drifted near Clara without looking at her. "Evening,"

he said to the air. His badge caught the last sun and then didn't.

Sam steered them down the side steps. "Eyes up," he said. "We're not special, but we're interesting."

They cut through the lot. The gray sedan idled half a block away. Nash leaned on a light pole and pretended to read a poster about a pancake feed.

"Still want tomorrow?" Sam asked when they reached the car.

"I want the truth," Clara said. "I don't want a story they wrote for me."

"Then we bring our own paper," he said. "We pick the spot across from the clinic—open ground, eyes on, exits clear. You won't be there alone, even if it looks like it. If they push for inside, we don't go in."

"Deal," she said, and felt how much the word cost.

Back at the motel, the room held the day's heat the way small rooms do. Sam spread a town map on the table and drew a simple plan: his car here, Lou's truck two blocks off, a clear line to the clinic door, a fallback path to the library lot. "No heroics," he said. "We're not there to catch anyone. We're there to see and to keep you whole."

Clara set the Room 12 key beside the map. **12** gleamed like a fact that refused to tell the rest of its sentence. "What if they don't show?"

"Then we keep pressing where paper leaves marks," Sam

said. "Marla's filing a request in the morning. Tom's digging in boxes with labels no one has read in years. Lou's chasing that plate and the initials on the calendar photo."

Her phone buzzed. **Unknown:** *Don't bring police. Don't bring copies. If you care about him, you'll come right.*

Clara typed a reply and erased it. She felt the small swing between fear and anger and chose neither, for now.

Sam slid an envelope across the table. "Burner," he said. "My number only. If your phone goes dark, use this. If anyone grabs it, drop it."

"Copy," she said, and slipped it into her pocket.

He stood. "I'll sit the lot. Sleep if you can."

"Do you ever?" she asked.

"On years that end in even numbers," he said, and let a smile move the corner of his mouth.

When he left, the AC tried and failed to make the room new. Clara stacked the folder, the map, the key. She walked to the door and checked the chain twice without thinking.

A soft slide sounded at the threshold. Something had been pushed under.

She picked it up. A white envelope, no stamp, no name. Inside, a single glossy print. A black-and-white image in a dark oval, the kind that makes its point without letters. At the edge, half cut off, a date in the corner: **OCT 2010**.

Clara sat on the bed and held the photo by its edges. The

grain crawled if she stared too long. She put the picture in a sleeve and added it to the folder without letting it touch the other pages.

Her phone buzzed. **Unknown:** *Tomorrow. 9 p.m. Blue door. Come right, or we're done being careful.*

She sent Sam a photo of the envelope and the print. *Under my door. No sender.*

Sam: *Got it. We don't blink. See you in the morning. Plan holds.*

She wrote in her notebook by the lamp's thin light:

- **Vote:** passed 4–2 with chair.

- **Pressure:** more texts; envelope with **Oct 2010** image slid under door.

- **Plan:** meet on our ground; no inside; eyes on.

She closed the book and slid it under the map. The motel hummed like a cheap fridge. Somewhere on the freeway a truck downshifted and found its gear.

Clara lay back and watched the ceiling. She pictured the blue door and the small square of concrete in front of it— the place where two people could stand without touching and still be tied to each other by a thin line. She pictured the print's dark oval and the tiny date trying to be neutral.

Sleep came in steps. When it finally took her, a voice in the back of a room said a line in a tone that didn't care what it broke: **Conrad will handle it.**

CHAPTER 11
The Sting

Chapter 11
The Sting

Dusk came on like a held breath. The wind went down to a whisper and the streetlights blinked awake one by one. Clara sat with Sam in the sedan across from the clinic, the map folded to a square on her knee. The blue door at Sage Crest Lodge faced the lot under a tired sodium lamp. Room 12 stamped in metal.

Sam ran through the plan once more. "You stop on the concrete square. Two minutes, max. If they push for inside, you say no. If someone tries a hand, you drop the envelope and step back. I'm twenty yards out. Lou is at the corner in the truck. Marla's on call."

Clara patted the decoy in her bag—a blank copy sleeve with the weight of paper and nothing else. The real folder sat in the motel safe with a note on it that said **no**.

Her phone buzzed. **Unknown:** *Now. Blue door. Alone.*

"Showtime," Sam said. He handed her the burner. "Mine is the only number in there. Hit once for call, twice for record."

"Copy," she said.

"Eyes up," he added. "No speeches. Let the silence do the work."

She slipped the burner into her pocket and double-tapped it.

Clara crossed the street with her hands where anyone could see them. Gravel underfoot. Air cooled fast in the shadow of the building. She stopped at the square of concrete in front of Room **12** and felt the strange stillness that comes when a lot remembers it's a stage.

The door didn't open. A shape moved at the end of the balcony rail, then another on the stairs. A man came down, slow, one hand on the rail like he wanted to look casual and landed on careful instead.

"Evening," he said. **Brett Sutter**, deputy—mid-thirties, clean jaw, a face that always looked one joke ahead. No badge showing. No hat.

"You picked a door," Clara said.

"Door's fine," he said, voice light. "Lobbies make people nervous." He stopped just out of arm's reach. "You bring what you got?"

"I brought questions," she said.

He smiled like he appreciated the effort. "Questions don't buy peace." His eyes flicked past her shoulder and came back. "Look, Ms. Hart, nobody wants a mess this week. You have pages you don't understand. We have friends who worry about the story those pages could tell if someone drew the wrong line between dots."

"Your friends have names," Clara said.

"Everybody has names," he said. "Not everybody needs them on paper."

"Who sent you?"

He didn't answer. He held out his hand. "Let me carry that

for you."

She kept the decoy under her arm. "Tell your friends they can send their concern to counsel."

He laughed once—a small, mean sound. "Lawyers are where we go when we've already lost." His eyes went to the number plate. "Blue suits you."

"Room twelve suited my husband," she said, and watched his face for the twitch you can't teach.

Nothing, until a flick at the mouth. "Accidents happen on bad roads," he said. "Everybody knows that."

"Then why are we here?"

He sat on his heels, then rose again, as if testing weight. "Because some folks like to keep the past where it belongs. Not in a meeting. Not in a paper. Not on a mic at council." He nodded at the envelope. "We'll make it easy. You hand that over. We hand you peace and quiet. Foundation sends a little help for your time. That's how towns stay towns."

"Peace and quiet," she said. "Is that what you called it on **March 3, 2016?**"

His eyes flashed and were flat again. "Careful."

Clara let the silence sit until he had to fill it. He took a step closer that put him where she could smell his aftershave. "Come inside," he said. "Somebody would like to say a word."

"No," she said.

He took another half step. "Don't be difficult."

On the far side of the lot, a gray sedan rolled past the entrance and parked two spaces down from the stairs, nose out. The driver's visor hung low. Clara kept the blue door behind her shoulder where the small peephole could see the top of her head if anyone looked.

"You brought company," she said.

Sutter didn't turn. "You brought yours," he said. "Fair's fair." He held out his hand again, palm up, the way a man holds a treat for a skittish dog. "Last ask."

Clara let the decoy envelope slide down into his palm. He tucked it once with his thumb, like a man testing a bill, then slipped it inside his jacket. "Good choice," he said.

A phone buzzed in his pocket. He glanced, then angled the screen away. "We're done." He stepped back.

"Tell your friends I don't sell my name," Clara said.

He snorted. "Everybody sells something. Some people don't know the price."

He turned toward the stairs. Halfway up, he paused and looked back down at her. "You should stop chasing ghosts, Ms. Hart. Sometimes they turn around."

He kept going. At the top, he knocked once on the Room **12** and didn't wait. The door opened a crack and closed again. A thin slice of light cut the rail and went out.

Clara stood until the skin on her arms stopped trying to

crawl off. Then she walked back across the lot like she had nowhere to be.

Sam met her at the curb and didn't touch her. "You okay?"

"I'm mad," she said. "That feels like being okay with teeth."

"Decoy's gone. Good," he said. "Lou?"

Lou's truck clicked once. His voice came through Sam's earbud: "Gray sedan plate confirms the shell. Back seat had a radio. Two heat signatures in Room **12** for about five minutes. One left by the back stair. Other stayed. I have a face on **Sutter**. No prize for the second."

"Copy," Sam said. To Clara: "You gave him nothing and got him to take a walk. That's a win."

"It doesn't feel like one," she said.

"It will when we play the tape," he said. "You got his lines?"

She pulled the burner and played back the thin room air and Sutter's voice asking for peace, for quiet, for inside. "It's not a confession," she said.

"It's a rope," Sam said. "We tie it to the other rope we have and see who trips."

Back at the motel, Sam spread the map again and marked Xs on the lot. "Two inside. One leaving by the back stair is a tell. Whoever stayed didn't want a camera catching their walk."

Clara slid the **Oct 2010** print to the corner of the table and stared at the dark oval until it was only shape. "They used to send pictures like this to make people feel less alone," she said. "Now they send them to make you feel watched."

Her phone buzzed. **Unknown:** *You made it worse. Tomorrow, last chance. Blue door. Alone.*

She set the phone face down and wrote in the notebook.

What I Know

- Sutter took the decoy. Tried to pull me inside.

- Gray sedan ran cover; radio in back seat.

- Two in **12**. One left by back stair.

What I Think

- The one who stayed wanted my face at their door on camera.

- If they have the **Patient copy**, they think I don't.

Sam watched her write. "We're going to nudge them," he said. He took out a single sheet he'd typed before they left: **Notice of Evidence Preservation — Clinic Records & Vault Logs** with Marla's letterhead. "I'll slide this to Paige and one to the council clerk. No names, just nouns. It'll shake the tree."

Clara exhaled. "And we wait."

"We wait," he said. "And we move the board."

Near midnight, the motel lot went quiet. Trucks on the freeway thinned to a rumor. Clara brushed her teeth, turned off the lamp, and stood at the window with the curtain barely open. The gray sedan sat dark, then rolled without lights, then stopped again in the shadow of a palm like a child hiding behind a pole.

The burner vibrated once. A new text lit the old phone.

Unknown: *No more notes. Bring what you have. You won't need it after.*

Clara typed *No* and erased it. She typed *Name yourself* and erased that, too. She let the message stay unanswered and set the phone on the table.

The room's air shifted. She felt it the way a person feels weather change through an old wall. A soft scuff sounded at the door.

"Sam?" she called, quiet.

Silence. Then a whisper that wasn't his, right at the seam where door met jamb.

"Clara?"

She froze. The voice was a woman's—thin with nerves, older than a girl, familiar to a place in her memory she couldn't place right away.

Clara moved to the door and put her mouth close to the wood. "Who is it?"

A breath. "You don't know me. You know my name."

"Say it," Clara whispered.

A pause like a coin balancing on its edge. "**Emily.**"

Clara's hand found the chain without looking. "I can't open this."

"I know," the voice said. "Don't. They're watching." A paper slipped under the door and stopped against Clara's foot. "He didn't—" The voice shook and found ground. "He was helping me. That's all I can say here."

Clara pressed her palm to the wood. "Where?"

"Tomorrow. **Dawn.** Old water tower. Come with the man who looks tired." A shaky breath. "No police cars."

"Wait," Clara said. "Are you safe?"

Silence. Then: "For now." Feet moved away—soft, fast, practiced.

Clara pulled the paper from the floor. A small note card, no print, one line in block letters that looked like someone trying to make their hand into a mask: **HE SAVED ME.**

She took a photo and sent it to Sam with two words: *She's alive.*

His reply came from the lot before the message landed: *On my way up. Don't open.*

She put the card in a sleeve and slid it into the folder. Then she wrote in her notebook.

What I Know

- **Emily** came to the door. Told me Andrew was helping.

- Meet: **dawn**, old water tower. No cruisers.

What I Think

- Voss and Hale didn't send that.

- Tomorrow isn't about a trade. It's about keeping a person standing long enough to speak.

Sam knocked—a tap they'd agreed on—and said his name. She checked the peephole, slid the chain, and let him in.

"She was here," Clara said. "She said his name without saying it."

Sam read the card and the text. He kept his face still. "We move early," he said. "We don't tell anyone who reports to Hale. We go quiet and wide."

Clara nodded. Her throat hurt. It felt like holding back a weather change. "If she's there," she said, "we keep her there."

"We keep her there," he said. "And we listen."

Outside, the gray sedan idled once more and then was gone. The night held. The blue door waited across the street like a dare someone had painted.

Clara turned off the lamp. The room settled. Sleep didn't come, but something like rest took its place—a thin layer, enough to walk on.

CHAPTER 12
Fallout

D awn came thin and colorless, the kind that makes edges look honest. The water tower stood on its hill like a tripod set to take the town's picture. Wind moved the weeds in slow tilts. A train sounded far off and then forgot what it was saying.

Clara and Sam parked below the dirt track and walked the last hundred yards on foot. No cruisers. No gray sedan. Sam's jacket was zipped against the morning and his eyes were busy without being loud.

"You talk first," he said, low. "I'll listen and keep watch."

Clara nodded. The steel of the tower felt cold even from a step away. She stood with her back to it and let the air find its shape.

A figure came out from the scrub, small and careful. A woman in a faded hoodie and a cap pulled low. She kept her hands where they could be seen. When she looked up, the face was thinner than the photo on the clinic wall, older at the edges, but it carried the same eyes.

"Emily," Clara said.

Emily took one more step and stopped. "You brought the tired man," she said. "Good." Her voice was hoarse but steady. "I can't be long."

Sam lifted a palm by way of hello and took a half step back to give the space to them.

"I can help if you let me," Clara said. "We need your words.

Your words keep you standing."

Emily's mouth tried at a smile and chose truth instead. "I'm not brave. I just ran out of places to hide." She looked past Clara at the tower, as if the rust might have advice. "I made a mess in 2010. I was twenty-two. He was nice to me. He made me feel seen. Then I was pregnant."

"Graham Voss," Clara said.

Emily nodded once. "I told him I was keeping the baby. He told me we'd 'handle it.' He said it like a meeting, like a budget. Then he stopped answering my calls. A week later a deputy came to my door and said there'd been a complaint about noise." She swallowed. "He stood in my kitchen and asked how far along I was. He said I would 'save us all trouble' if I took care of it."

"Sheriff Hale's man," Clara said.

"Not Nash," Emily said. "Younger. Jokes for a face. He said a name on the phone that day—Conrad. I remember because I thought I'd never met a Conrad." She took a breath that looked like it hurt. "I got scared. I packed a bag and drove to the high school lot because I didn't know where else to go. Andrew found me there. He was leaving the gym. He looked like a person who could hold weight. I asked him to help."

"What did he do?" Clara asked, the words soft so they wouldn't break.

"He gave me the spare room in the old bungalow he kept for tools. He paid cash for groceries so there wouldn't be a trail. He called a clinic in Reno for real prenatal care and drove me out of town in a truck with a bad radio so no one would see my car. He told me he didn't want you touched by any of it. He said he'd tell you when it was safe. I don't think he knew when that would be."

Clara put her hand on the steel behind her and let it take some of the shake. "And the night at the reservoir?"

"I was two months from due," Emily said. "Andrew said I needed to leave for a while. He set up a safe spot with a friend two towns over. We were going to move me after dark so no one would see. He went to get gas. When the sirens went by I thought... I thought maybe they were chasing the same storm that had been chasing me. In the morning I heard he was gone." She looked at Clara and didn't look away. "He didn't cheat on you. He didn't touch me like that. He helped me because I asked and because he couldn't watch the sheriff and a rich man make a person into a problem."

Clara felt the words land and settle. They didn't erase anything. They set it in order. "Where did you go?"

"North," Emily said. "A clinic finished the care. A friend of a friend took me in. When the baby came, I left him with a family that had a yard and quiet. I visit with letters. I don't sign them. I've lived small. People can live small a long time if they have to."

Sam stepped closer, gentle. "Emily, I'm Sam Reyes. I don't work for Sheriff Hale. I need to record you saying what you just told us. I'll take you to a lawyer who doesn't answer to him. We'll keep you safe. Do you understand?"

Emily's eyes flicked to the dirt road and back. "If I talk, do they stop?"

"We make it hard for them to keep going," Sam said. "That's the first stop."

She nodded. "Okay."

He tapped his phone and kept it below eye level. "Say your name for the record, the year you're talking about, and what Graham Voss and Sheriff Hale did or asked others to do."

Emily did. She kept her voice even. She told the dates—**October 2010** for the first clinic photo, **2011** for the birth, **March 2016** for the meeting in town when she heard the word "Conrad" and a promise to "keep it tight." She named **Brett Sutter** as the deputy who came to her kitchen. She named Voss as the man who told her to "take care of it." She said Andrew Hart helped her vanish and kept her safe and planned her move north. She said the word "murder" once and had to swallow.

Sam stopped the record and saved it in three places. He looked at Clara and then at Emily. "We go now," he said. "No hospital. No station. We go to an office with a locked file room and a woman whose job is to keep paper from being eaten."

Emily's hands shook once and were still again. "I have a bag that fits under a seat."

"Bring it," Sam said.

Marla opened her door in jeans and a sweater and didn't waste words. She set Emily at a table with water and a pen and made the room feel like there was more oxygen in it.

She took the phone from Sam and backed up the audio to a clean drive. She typed while Emily spoke, then printed, then read it back, and let Emily change a word that wasn't hers.

"Chain is clean," Marla said when the ink dried. "We'll get you to a quiet place today. You'll only have two names: mine and Sam's. Everyone else will go through me. Sam?" She didn't have to finish the question.

"I'm going to the state's office two counties over," he said. "They don't owe Hale. Lou will hand them the phone clips and the March audio. The council clerk has our preservation notice. The bank has the logs on hold. We have enough cords to make a knot."

Marla nodded. "I'll file for a temporary order to keep the sheriff's office from contacting Ms. Lane under cover of a welfare check." She looked at Emily. "You'll be 'Ms. Lane' here, for now."

Emily nodded, grateful for the small distance a false name can make.

Clara watched the pages stack. She felt something inside her ease its grip a fraction and then hang on again. "What about Voss?" she asked. "What about Sutter?"

"Pieces first," Marla said. "Then the table."

The state office sat in a low building that used to be a bank. Sam waited in a windowless room with a scuffed conference table and told his story to a woman who listened like a metronome—steady, counting beats. He slid over the audio with the **March 2016** timestamps, the phone files with Sutter asking for "peace and quiet," the photo of the calendar with **Mar 3 — Civic Rm — GV/CH/BS**, the bank letter holding the safe-deposit logs, the notice to the *Chronicle* and the city clerk. He kept Hale's name where it belonged. He kept Voss's name where it belonged.

By noon a judge signed a narrow order that let the state pick up a phone from a pocket that wasn't theirs and speak to a sheriff in a voice he had to answer. It wasn't a grand moment. Paper slid. A stamp came down. People stood.

Sam called Clara from the parking lot. "They're moving," he said. "I'm going to speak with Hale before the state does. He'll talk to me if he's going to talk to anyone."

"Be careful," she said.

"I'm good at careful," he said, and tried a smile she could hear.

Hale's office had a window that liked to catch late light. It didn't have any of that now. He sat behind the desk with his hands flat as if they were making a promise to the wood.

"You're early," he said when Sam stepped in. "I was told to expect the state."

"You're getting them," Sam said. "I came first because you've still got a choice about how this looks."

Hale's face didn't move much, but something in the room did. "You think you know something."

"I know enough," Sam said. "I know you were in a room in

March 2016 when Voss said the council was 'tight' and a problem needed to stop wandering. I know someone said 'Conrad will handle it.' I know your deputy Sutter tried to bring a widow inside a motel room and asked for peace and quiet in exchange for paper. I know an Emily with a son in another zip code just signed a statement that ties your donor crush to a threat and your office to a follow-through."

Hale looked past Sam to the wall and then back, as if the wood might help the math. "You don't know what you think you know."

"Maybe," Sam said. "But a state attorney is about to stand where I'm standing. You can tell them you were a cop who got used by a man with money, or you can tell them you were the man with the idea. One picture ends with you in a smaller room less long."

Silence. The kind that comes when a person is trying not to hear a clock. Hale rubbed his thumb along a scar on the desk that had been filled and sanded and still wanted to be a scar.

"Voss made a call," he said at last. "He made a lot of calls. Things got said in rooms. Lines got crossed. Sutter likes to be a problem. You going to give me a deal?"

"I'm not the one who writes deals," Sam said. "But I can put a note in the file that says who spoke first and who kept speaking."

Hale's jaw worked once. "You want a name to go with 'Conrad.'"

"I want you to tell the truth," Sam said.

Hale's eyes went to the window that didn't have light and came back tired. "Conrad Pike. Voss's fixer. Not on payroll, not on paper. He made messes into absences." He swallowed. "I signed things I shouldn't have. I told myself I was keeping order. The man drove this town like it was a truck with his name on the title. You think you can stop that by writing a nice letter?"

"I think we just did," Sam said. "State's at your door."

As if on cue, a knock came. Two people in suits stepped in and filled the room with a third kind of air. Hale sat back. He looked like a man who had found his chair too late.

Voss didn't get a speech on the steps. The state took him at his office, where the glass looked out on a map of the town he had drawn in his head. He was forty-five and dressed like a man in a magazine. He asked if there was a misunderstanding. They said there was paperwork. He smiled for the hall camera and then didn't.

Paige's update on the *Chronicle* site was clipped and clean: **Businessman Detained; Sheriff Cooperates in State Review.** The comments did what comments do—cheered, sneered, asked what took so long, made it about someone's uncle. The Foundation posted a note about pausing promotional activity "out of respect for community process." The council clerk, who wore cardigans and never raised her voice, put a line on the agenda for "Reconsideration — Promenade."

Marla called Clara from the quiet place where Emily was getting a sandwich and a shower. "She's holding," Marla said. "She wanted me to tell you thank you without making a scene of it."

"Tell her thank you back," Clara said. "And that she doesn't owe anyone a story at a microphone."

"She doesn't," Marla said. "You don't either. But I think we do owe Andrew an answer on paper."

Clara looked at the folder on the table, at the **Room 12 stamp** on the motel key she still carried out of habit. "We will."

They went to the reservoir at dusk with no speeches and no crowd. Sam stood by while Clara walked the gravel to the guardrail and set a small stone on the post. She didn't say a prayer. She said Andrew's name like it was a door she was opening for the first time without knocking.

"I thought you were somewhere small," she said to the water. "It turns out you were holding up the part of the sky over somebody else." She let the wind take the rest.

Sam came up beside her and didn't fill the silence. After a while he said, "Hale's giving it all up. Sutter has counsel and less swagger. Voss's people are suddenly bad at returning calls. The state will talk to a grand jury. It won't be quick. But the center moved."

Clara nodded. "Will they say it out loud? About Andrew?"

"They will," Sam said. "We'll make sure they do."

They walked back to the car. Clara took out her notebook on the hood and wrote three lines.

What I Know

- Emily is alive. Andrew helped her. He didn't cheat. He chose to keep a person safe.

- Hale flipped. Voss is in a room with people who don't owe him.

- Paper holds when you put enough hands on it.

She closed the book and set her palm on the cover until the heat from her hand felt like it had gone somewhere useful.

The next morning, Paige ran a short item with a quote from the state: **Evidence indicates Mr. Hart's death was not consistent with an accident; further review is underway.** It wasn't poetry. It was something better. It was a record.

Clara read it once and didn't need to read it again. She walked to the kitchen, poured coffee, and took it to the porch. The wind was mild. A moth tapped the light and then thought better of it.

Sam texted: *You okay?*

Getting there, she wrote.

Want a drive?

Later. I'm going to write a few things down first.

She set her cup on the rail and opened the notebook one

more time. Under **What I Think**, she drew a single line and wrote in the space below it:

- **SC** on Andrew's calendar was both things—**Silver Crown** and **Sage Crest**. The town he tried to keep honest, and the door where someone wanted me to forget how.

She closed the notebook and put it on the table. She slid the motel key into an envelope and wrote **Return** on the front. She took the **Oct 2010** print from its sleeve and set it in a separate folder labeled **Clinic** for Marla to keep. She touched the unsent letter one more time and put it where it wasn't the first thing in a drawer.

When she stepped outside, the light had the thin, honest quality it gets before the day decides its mood. She locked the door and put the keys in her pocket and walked toward town at a pace that didn't apologize. A car passed and didn't slow. A dog barked and gave up. The wind carried dust and a hint of water and something like a new start that didn't need to be called that.

Clara turned the corner and saw the blue door in her mind, and for the first time since she came back, it didn't ask anything of her.

Epilogue

Two weeks later, the Promenade banner sat folded in the clerk's office and the agenda carried a plain line: Reconsideration — Promenade. The state announced charges against Graham Voss—conspiracy and witness tampering among them—and said the sheriff was cooperating. Brett Sutter was placed on leave pending review. A warrant named Conrad Pike. Paige's brief on the Chronicle site ran a single, square sentence: Records now show Andrew Hart did not die by accident; further action is pending. It wasn't grand. It was the record turning the right way.

On a cool morning, Marla walked a quiet block behind a small park while Clara sat with Emily on a bench within sight. Emily had a new name and a safer address. She would see her son the right way, in the right rooms, on paper that couldn't be taken back. "No more knocking after midnight," Emily said, and managed a smile that looked like a beginning. Clara squeezed her hand once and let go.

Before she left the motel for good, Clara slid the Room **12** key across the counter and watched the clerk drop it in a box. Back home, she opened her notebook and wrote one last line: **What I Know** — Andrew kept a person safe when it was hard. She closed the cover and breathed in the thin, honest morning light. The blue door, in her mind, was only paint again, and the reservoir held the sky without asking anything back.

THE END...

Made in United States
Cleveland, OH
19 September 2025

20314023R00075